MISS BIANCA
in the Orient

Illustrated by

Erik Blegvad

MISS BIANCA
in the Orient

by Margery Sharp

A YEARLING BOOK

Published by
Dell Publishing Co., Inc.
1 Dag Hammarskjold Plaza
New York, New York 10017

Text copyright © 1970 by Margery Sharp
Illustrations copyright © 1970 by Erik Blegvad

Yearling ® TM 913705, Dell Publishing Co., Inc.

ISBN: 0-440-45716-5

Reprinted by arrangement with Little, Brown and
Company (Inc.)

Printed in the United States of America

Fourth Dell printing—December 1982

CW

Contents

MISS BIANCA
in the Orient

1. The Banquet

Miss Bianca sat before her mirror in the Porcelain Pagoda applying the discreetest possible touch of pomade to her whiskers. (Unusually in a white mouse they were dark brown, like her equally unusual dark brown eyes.) She had already applied the discreetest possible touch of rose-water behind each ear; she was making a rather special toilet. Her ermine fur, brushed and brushed, shone like silver; her silver necklace, polished and polished, gleamed like dewdrops — or like her beautifully

3

polished tiny nails. Her tail was practically coiffured. Miss Bianca never looked anything else than extremely elegant, but on this particular occasion she looked quite ravishing!

So certainly thought her dear old friend Bernard, as she emerged to greet him beside the Venetian glass fountain in the Pagoda's small encircling pleasure ground. The whole establishment was situated in the schoolroom of an Embassy, which was one reason why Miss Bianca, in addition to her duties as Perpetual Madam President of the Mouse Prisoners' Aid Society, had almost too many social engagements. Bernard, the Society's hardworking Secretary, never went out at all; but if he always came to see Miss Bianca off to a party it wasn't through envy. It was because he admired her so in evening dress.

"What's on tonight?" asked Bernard interestedly.

"Just another banquet," said Miss Bianca, "in honor of some newly accredited Ambassador. I only hope there won't be too many speeches!"

She sighed. She wasn't showing off — Miss Bianca never showed off, she was too well bred — but this was actually her third banquet within a week. The Boy, the Ambassador's son, her patron and playmate, was only just old enough to stay up for them, and badly needed Miss Bianca in his pocket to lend moral support. (To be truthful, Miss Bianca sometimes gave him a gentle nip as well, if he looked like nodding.)

"And tomorrow's the General Meeting," said Bernard anxiously. "Do try and get home early, Miss Bianca!"

Miss Bianca sighed again. Since giving up the active role of Madam Chairwoman, General Meetings of the M.P.A.S. rather bored her. As Perpetual Madam President, she felt her position too purely decorative. But all the members liked to see her on the platform — the famous Miss Bianca, leader of how many daring expeditions! * — and to hear her famous silvery voice, if only introducing a speaker. So Miss Bianca always did her duty by a General Meeting, just as she did by an Ambassadorial banquet, though she would have much preferred to stay at home writing poetry. Her first slim volume of verse had gone into three editions.

Bernard said he'd hang on at the Pagoda anyway, just to see she got back safely; and with that Miss Bianca ran off to join the Boy, waiting to put her in his pocket. It contained already a few salted almonds, so that Miss Bianca could have a little banquet of her own. — She brushed her whiskers against his thumb in acknowledgement of the kind thought.

"I do hope you won't find it dreadfully dull, Miss Bianca," said the Boy, "and I do think it's nice of you to come!"

Who could have imagined that this was to be the start of one of the most perilous adventures even Miss Bianca had ever undertaken!

* A Norwegian poet rescued from the Black Castle, the child Patience from the Diamond Palace, Teddy-Age-Eight from the Salt Mines.

5

2

Actually she found the banquet quite enjoyable. She had always an eye for the picturesque, and peeping out of the Boy's pocket was delighted to observe the new Ambassador, from some Oriental state, attired in ceremonial robes of Oriental splendor. His cloth-of-gold and emeralds threw just run-of-the-mill satins and diamonds, and even Orders and other decorations, quite in the shade! Another piece of picturesqueness was the beautiful letter of credentials he had brought: all the communications that really mattered, between his own and other embassies, were typed, so that carbons could be kept; this particular communication being a purely formal expression of politeness, the Ambassador offered across the dinner table half-a-dozen lines of Oriental script elegantly brushed on rice-paper and contained in a padded silk pouch embroidered with seed-pearls. Every lady present exclaimed admiringly, and wanted the pouch for a handkerchief-sachet — but of course the Boy's mother, as hostess, had first claim.

"Though the contents must be strictly the property of His Excellency," smiled the new Ambassador (all Ambassadors are called Excellencies, to encourage them to be excellent), "if so gracious a lady cares to accept such a mere trifle as the envelope, my country will be honored indeed!"

The Boy's mother smiled back. — She was looking

particularly beautiful herself that night, in pale blue lace and an aquamarine tiara; in fact Miss Bianca strongly suspected that even if she *hadn't* been hostess, His Excellency would have found some excuse for giving her that pouch everyone wanted!

"You must permit me to send a little gift in turn, to your Ranee," said she. (Ranee is the Oriental for queen.) "Would Her Highness accept, do you think, this trifling thimble?"

For a good Ambassadress, like a good Boy Scout, is always prepared. The thimble the Boy's mother had slipped into her evening bag (just in case) was gold rimmed with opals — actually a gift from, and fit for, a queen. To be sure, it wasn't very practical, because as the Ambassadress had discovered, any embroidery-silk always tangled on the opals; but it was still extremely pretty and precious — so why should the Oriental Ambassador frown?

"To be truthful, dear lady," said he, in a lowered voice (they were naturally sitting next to each other, so a little private conversation was possible), "Her Highness's requirements in the way of sables, silver foxes and an ermine bedspread ready-made-up absolutely fill all baggage-space on the plane that must reluctantly bear me away from you — taking precedence," he added, frowning again, "even over sacks of seeds! And if you ask how little weighs even a golden thimble, I can only answer that Her Highness has never employed a thimble in her life; the pouch you so much admire indeed came from the

Palace, but it was embroidered by one of her ladies . . .
In fact," murmured the Ambassador, lowering his voice
still further, "our highly ornamental Ranee is one of
those anachronisms every new republic has to live with
— but I can assure you that in all essentials the Palace
and the Capital are worlds apart!"

"How understandable!" murmured the Ambassadress
tactfully; then smiled again — smiling, at banquets, being *de rigueur*. "Since I mayn't offer a thimble — and
you spoke of seeds — what about a packet of mustard-
and-cress?"

"Accepted with pleasure!" declared the Oriental Ambassador, now smiling too. So did all the other ladies
smile, diplomatically concealing their disappointment;
to make up for which the Ambassador was so particularly charming to each in turn, all agreed in the drawing-
room afterwards that he had the nicest manners possible!

"And I shall keep his pouch for my very nicest hand-
kerchieves!" said the Boy's mother.

But the Boy had a different plan. As soon as everyone
was gone, he pulled Miss Bianca gently out of his pocket
and sat her down on the seed-pearl-embroidered square
of silk. Has it been mentioned that the silk was pink? It
was; Miss Bianca's favorite pale rose-color. Against it
her silvery fur showed up precisely but with extreme
delicacy; the biggest pearl was just the right size to fit
into the curve of her tail . . .

"Oh, do let's give it to Miss Bianca!" begged the Boy.
"I'm sure she'd like to have it in the Porcelain Pagoda!

Just think how cozy she could be, tucked up inside, when it's cold!"

His mother the Ambassadress bent over them affectionately. She had the highest opinion of Miss Bianca, who besides keeping the Boy awake at banquets also sat regularly on his shoulder to help him learn his lessons. It was actually the Ambassadress who had given Miss Bianca her silver chain.

"Why, I really meant to keep such a pretty thing myself," said she, lightly fingering the beautiful seed-pearl embroidery. "But as Miss Bianca looks so charming on it, hers it shall be!"

Miss Bianca gracefully bowed her thanks. At the Ambassadress's bidding a footman carefully carried the pouch, Miss Bianca still reclining on it, off to the schoolroom, and set it down inside the Pagoda's pleasure ground, while the Boy went to bed.

3

"Good gracious me!" exclaimed Bernard — who as will be remembered was waiting for Miss Bianca's return. "Whatever's *that?*"

"A gift from the Orient," explained Miss Bianca complacently. "Don't you think, my dear Bernard, it will afford a most delightful winter retreat?"

Bernard walked all round the pink silk square admiringly.

"Just the job," he agreed. "Either in your boudoir or

out here in the grounds. Why, you could sit in it out of doors, and enjoy any sun, all through winter!"

"Exactly what *I* thought," said Miss Bianca. "Of course I haven't seen inside yet, but the lining also appears to be of silk, which always promotes comfort. Seed-pearls, inside, I confess I could do without — they're so bumpy!"

"Let's look inside now," said Bernard eagerly.

He helped Miss Bianca down, and together they raised the embroidered flap. ("Put it up on poles, and you'd have an awning!" suggested Bernard.) Then they pushed apart the silken walls within. These were not pink, but cream, and smelled sweetly of attar-of-roses. A few large needle-holes where the pearls were sewn on afforded perfect ventilation even at the back. There was in fact nothing to mar Miss Bianca's new little nest of comfort and beauty — save that it was occupied already . . .

There in the furthest silk-lined corner lay coiled — a serpent!

2. Ali

F̲OR A DREADFUL̲ moment Bernard and Miss Bianca
stood frozen in horror. One thing they both knew about
serpents was that some of them eat mice. Then Bernard
pounced. — Though never a success in society, lacking
the art of easy chitchat, he possessed other, more valuable qualities. He was wonderfully stouthearted, and ever
prompt in action. The serpent was in fact a very small
one; scarcely a snake; rather a snakeling, about four
inches long and a pretty green color, but even had it been
a boa constrictor or python, Bernard in defense of Miss
Bianca would have pounced just the same. Not fear, but

excitement, made him miss his mark; instead of seizing the intruder by the throat, he landed sitting on its tail. The serpent, or snakeling, sneezed.

"I suppose you haven't a thermometer?" it asked anxiously. "I have to watch my temperature; I'm rather delicate."

All animals speak a universal animal language, besides their own, so though the accent was strange Bernard and Miss Bianca had no difficulty in understanding, and the homely words did much to calm their fears.

"I have no doubt there is one in the Ambassador's bathroom," said Miss Bianca. "(Bernard, do get off his tail!) But might one ask — purely as a matter of form — whence and why you are here, also what is your name?"

("I should jolly well think we might!" growled Bernard, without moving.

"How would *you* like a stranger sitting on *your* tail?" rebuked Miss Bianca. Then Bernard moved.)

"Ali," said the snake, as soon as Bernard's weight was off gliding out into the pleasure ground and stretching. "My name is Ali, and why I'm here I suppose is because I felt a cold coming on. It looked just the place," he explained, with a wistful backward glance at the padded silken walls, "to keep away from draughts in . . . So I slipped inside and went to sleep, and when I woke up a whole wad of paper had been pushed under the flap — absolutely *all* draughts excluded! — and I felt so comfy I went to sleep again. But *where* do I wake up?"

"I fear far, far from home," said Miss Bianca compassionately. "Your home being doubtless the Orient?"

"Well, of course," said Ali. "Isn't *this* the Orient?"

Miss Bianca and Bernard exchanged speaking looks. The country to which the Boy's father was Ambassador was so *un*-Oriental, winter lasted six months. On its mountains, snow lay all the year round . . .

"However unwittingly, you have traveled by air," explained Miss Bianca, "also I fear to a very different climate."

"You'll probably freeze to death," added Bernard hopefully.

Ali sneezed again; then like many persons who have landed themselves in awkward situations, put the blame on someone else.

"It's all that wretched page boy's fault," he complained. "I *thought* he had a cold. Then I thought he was just sniveling as usual, so out of sheer kindheartedness I let him pick me up and stroke me. Now besides catching it I've been forced to travel (you tell me) by air to a completely unsuitable climate where I shall probably get pneumonia as well. I'd better go to bed at once."

"Not here you won't," said Bernard. "This happens to be a lady's private residence."

He looked at Miss Bianca eagerly, ready at a twitch of her whiskers to run the intruder out. But Miss Bianca's attention, and though she was by this time quite as disgusted as Bernard by Ali's effrontery, had been preliminarily caught. She was so fond of her own Boy, the mention of any boy whatever always interested her.

"What page boy?" asked Miss Bianca.

"Why, the Ranee's," said Ali. ("I suppose you don't mind my just sitting *down?*" he added to Bernard — at the same time making free of one of Miss Bianca's garden-chairs.) "That is, he *used* to be Her Highness's page; now he's in the elephant lines waiting to be trampled to smithereens at next full moon — all on account of his sniveling so! Believe it or not, he actually sniveled into Her Highness's sherbet!"

There was a slight pause, while Miss Bianca with her right-hand set of whiskers signaled Bernard to keep quiet and with the left-hand set expressed compassionate emotion.

"If by sniveling you mean crying," said she, "why did he cry?"

"Ask me another," said Ali carelessly. "Of course he's an orphan: his parents I believe were some sort of medical missionaries, from some quite foreign country, but when *they* died Her Highness was good enough to receive him as a page. She even designed his costume herself — white satin, with a cherry-colored sash!"

"Enough to console *any* child for the loss of his parents!" agreed Miss Bianca sweetly — but of course meaning the exact opposite. (This is known as irony.) Bernard, more forthright, was about to exclaim that if Ali thought any decent boy could be consoled for anything by having a pink sash tied round his tum then Ali didn't know much about boys; but the latter spoke again first.

"Another thing the little idiot sniveled about was want-

ing to do lessons," he recalled. "Can you imagine anything so ungrateful, when his whole life when he wasn't
fetching and carrying was simply a round of pleasure!
He *deserved* trampling," said Ali, "I suppose you haven't
such a thing as a hot water bottle?"

"No, we haven't!" almost shouted Bernard.

"You needn't be *brutal* about it," complained Ali. "I'm
not poisonous. In fact I think poison's rather vulgar. I'm
perfectly harmless, and all that sort of thing. In fact,
I'm so particularly sweet-natured, even if you won't give
me a bed I shan't hiss a hiss."

With which he settled himself more comfortably in
Miss Bianca's best garden-chair and went to sleep again.

2

"Well!" exclaimed Bernard. "I never thought much of
reptiles, but this one takes the cake. Whatever do we do
now?"

"Put a rug over him," said Miss Bianca practically.

"*I'd* turn the fountain on him," said Bernard.

"Then he probably *would* get pneumonia, and thus
become more of a liability than ever," pointed out Miss
Bianca, moving toward the Pagoda, "whereas after a good
warm night's rest he may awake perfectly fit."

"Not Ali," said Bernard. "If he hasn't a cold he'll have
something else. I wouldn't be surprised if he deliberately
came out in spots. — Bring *two* rugs, Miss Bianca; one
for me as well, because I'm going to keep watch. I'm not

going to leave you all alone here with a snake in your grass!"

It was a strange sight indeed that the moon through the schoolroom window shone upon: Ali curled in one garden-chair under one rug alongside Bernard in another under another. But Ali's covering was just a plain sort of blanket-rug, whereas Bernard's was Miss Bianca's own *couvre-pied* (pale pink silk stuffed with swansdown) off her own chaise-longue and smelling deliciously of her own special rose-water. If only Bernard could have felt sure Miss Bianca was going to forget about the Ranee's page, he would have spent the happiest night of his life.

Only of course Miss Bianca, being Miss Bianca, didn't.

3

"In the morning," meditated Miss Bianca, combing her whiskers, "Ali and I must have a really serious talk; for doubtless he will return, as he came, with the Ambassador; and that's only in a couple of days' time, and the full moon at least a fortnight off. Who knows," thought Miss Bianca, brushing her tail, "but that the Ranee is less cruel than Ali presents her — only Orientally thoughtless? A word in season might arouse her better nature; and I'm sure Ali is ideally placed to give it — evidently a familiar of the Palace, and I dare say quite a pet! 'Tis true he takes the dreadful affair very lightly," thought Miss Bianca, slipping between her pink silk

sheets, "and one could wish he showed a little more back-bone; but if one can't appeal to his heart or courage, I'm sure one may to his vanity and self-importance! I'll coach him thoroughly tomorrow," decided Miss Bianca, laying head to pillow, "in some touching little speech, perhaps with actions, and I'm sure I can persuade him!"

Miss Bianca could have persuaded a fox to turn aside from a hen-coop. It was on record in the M.P.A.S. Year-book how she'd once persuaded a cat called Mamelouk not to eat Bernard. She had persuaded even bloodhounds to think of their mothers. She thus (though in all modesty) felt little doubt of being able to persuade Ali to play his part, when it was carefully explained to him next morning.

The only hobble to this sensible plan was that in the morning, Ali wasn't there!

3. In the Conservatory

"I'M DREADFULLY SORRY, Miss Bianca," apologized Bernard, "but I must have gone to sleep."

He couldn't understand it. He hadn't even *tried* not to go to sleep — the hours after midnight being just the time when mice are by nature wide-awake and on the go. He'd even planned, if he got cramp, to do a little weeding in the Pagoda flower-beds. But Miss Bianca, through her association with the Boy, had come to adopt almost human hours, and Bernard, because he couldn't bear not to associate with Miss Bianca, had unconsciously done the same. So they were both, so to speak, up late, and it was small wonder that when Miss Bianca emerged next morning Bernard had been awake only just long enough to make a hasty and fruitless search of the grounds and surrounding schoolroom.

Though small wonder, it was still dreadfully unfortunate. Miss Bianca's expression, upon seeing Ali's chair empty, and Ali nowhere in view, was such that Bernard nearly took a header into the Venetian glass fountain. But that would have been cowardly (besides giving Miss Bianca a lot of bother if there had to be an inquest, and also he hadn't yet signed the codicil to his will leaving her his stamp collection), so he instead made the heartfelt apology described above, hopefully adding something about good riddance to bad rubbish.

"Actually I wished to speak to Ali rather particularly," said Miss Bianca. "Have you any idea where he may have gone?"

"Of course I've looked," said Bernard, "and I don't believe he's anywhere in the schoolroom. The trouble is, he's such a slippery little reptile, I suppose he could have gone anywhere . . ."

"If he's gone into the Boy's mother's dressing-room," said Miss Bianca, "I'm sorry, Bernard, but I shall never speak to you again!"

Bernard paled. — The fountain was but a mouse-jump away; no doubt Miss Bianca could get a doctor's certificate not to appear at the inquest, and would she really care for his stamp collection? As these thoughts rushed through Bernard's agitated mind — as Miss Bianca turned coldly away — he nearly did jump. — However, at this very moment, most fortunately, the footman bringing Miss Bianca's breakfast of cream cheese in a silver bonbon dish was heard to observe to the housemaid following with brush and pan that Thomas Gardener had seen a snake in the conservatory. "You don't tell me!" squealed the housemaid. "Goodness gracious, I'm glad *I* don't have to go in there!" "Only quite a small one," reassured the footman. "As one might say, or rather as Thomas Gardener says, even ornamental; light green."

2

"So *that*'s where he's got to!" exclaimed Bernard relievedly, as soon as he and Miss Bianca were alone again. "I suppose one might have expected it — just seeking his own amusement by slithering off to look at pot-plants!"

"Say rather, seeking his own temperature," corrected Miss Bianca. "Indeed I'm rather heartened by his showing so much initiative; it gives one better hopes of him. We must nonetheless rout him out, however, for as I said before I need to speak to him particularly."

Her manner remained cold.

It was still so early, Thomas Gardener had gone back to his own breakfast — far more substantial than Miss Bianca's: scrambled eggs on bacon topped off by a wing of cold chicken and a slice of pork pie — and Miss Bianca and Bernard had the conservatory to themselves. Unlike the former, who often strolled there with the Boy's mother, Bernard had never yet set foot within its

glazed doors, and even now scarcely appreciated the floral treasures spread before him. Surrounded by orchids of every variety, also camellias in full bloom and trailing stephanotis, all Bernard wanted to set eyes on was a slim green tail-tip (by now possibly spotted) he'd very much like to get his teeth into. Miss Bianca, on the other hand, couldn't help pausing so often in admiration, Bernard began to worry lest Thomas Gardener should return before they'd completed a proper search. — His fears were justified; only those who have looked for a needle in a haystack can estimate the difficulty of looking for a very small green snake in a very large, largely green, conservatory. A hundred dangling tendrils, a hundred exposed roots, might have been Ali, or at least a section of him! Only none, when Bernard impetuously pounced, was, and he'd never apologized to so many vegetables in his life before Miss Bianca's loitering gaze, not his own impatient one, at last detected their quarry.

"Pray cast your eye," murmured Miss Bianca, "at the roots of that extraordinarily beautiful *Cattelya cambriensis!*"

Only a tail-tip indeed protruded; yet somehow suggested, by its curve and immobility, that the owner had slithered in, and coiled himself round, and in the steamy heat, exquisitely canopied by orchids, gone to sleep again . . .

"Ali!" called Miss Bianca, in her most beguiling tones — but quite loudly.

There was no response.

Bernard gave the tail a slight nip. Still no response —
except that it retracted, which might have been no more
than a physical reaction.

"Oh, dear!" exclaimed Miss Bianca. "I do hope he
hasn't gone into *hibernation!*"

"I shouldn't be surprised," offered Bernard.

"It's too tiresome for words," said Miss Bianca, "when
I have so much of importance to discuss with him! Moreover, his Ambassador returns in but two days' time, and
how is Ali to travel in a state of complete coma? We
must at all costs rouse him!"

"And hold his head under the fountain?" suggested
Bernard eagerly.

"At a pinch, even that," said Miss Bianca, "and then
plenty of black coffee!"

But when they looked again, Ali, for the second time,
had totally disappeared. Peering into the hole, which
turned out to be quite deep, Bernard couldn't distinguish
even the faintest glimmer of the smallest light-green
scale . . .

"Let *me* look," said Miss Bianca.

"No, please don't, Miss Bianca," said Bernard hastily.
"I dare say, if he overheard, he's feeling pretty bad-
tempered; and after all we've only his own word for it
that he's nonpoisonous . . . It was my fault entirely,"
said brave Bernard, "and anyway it's no use just *looking;*
I'll go in after him."

There was a moment's pause. With mixed emotions,
Bernard saw Miss Bianca's whiskers tremble. Why they

were mixed was because he hated to see her in any sort of distress, but at the same time felt that despite her dreadful words about never speaking to him again, she still valued him too much to be indifferent to his risking snakebite.

"I dare say it'll be quite a *mild* sort of poison," said Bernard, more bravely still.

Lighter than a willow leaf, Miss Bianca's hand rested upon his arm . . .

"No, Bernard," said she. "The risk is too great."

"No? You really mean no?" almost shouted Bernard.

"The risk is too great," repeated Miss Bianca. "Also I begin to believe him too unreliable," she added, "for any useful purpose. Let us leave him to his own selfish devices, and forget him!"

Bernard's heart leapt. He didn't quite understand what she meant about Ali being unreliable, and didn't try to; all he knew was that Miss Bianca and he were friends again, and that was quite enough to make his heart not only leap, but practically somersault. It leapt all the way back to the schoolroom, and if Miss Bianca's manner was slightly preoccupied, Bernard was far too happy to notice.

"Now do please get a good rest this afternoon, Miss Bianca," said he, as they parted at the Pagoda gate. "You were up late last night, it's been a trying morning, and there's a M.P.A.S. General Meeting at one A.M. Of course you'll be on the platform?"

"Of course!" sighed Miss Bianca.

4. The General Meeting

As HAS BEEN said earlier, the Pepetual Madam President of the Mouse Prisoners' Aid Society had become rather bored by its General Meetings. She had attended so many! — and save for herself, no one ever seemed to put a motion of any interest! The motions put by Miss Bianca were indeed often interesting to the point of hair-raisingness, for she ever urged the Society on to the actual rescue of prisoners, whereas a large body of opinion was in favor of merely cheering them up. Led by Miss Bianca, the Ladies' Guild, the Boy Scouts, even a couple of University professors, had adventured into perils they liked to talk about afterwards, but hadn't at all enjoyed at the time; so it really wasn't surprising if the current mood was rather cautious. Most recent motions dealt with such projects as Meals-on-Wheels for Shut-ins; and of course shut-ins were in a sense prisoners too; but whoever, delivering a Meal-on-Wheels, reflected Miss Bianca, had been chased by bloodhounds?

"I must be careful not to set too much store by the picturesque!" Miss Bianca chided herself — and so, as has also been said, made a point of always attending every single General Meeting going.

2

These took place in the Moot-hall, a majestic building which had started life as a claret-cask, and which generations of mice had fitted out quite beautifully with rows of matchbox benches and a platform at one end. The platform itself was carpentered from cigar-box cedarwood, with upon it four walnut-shell chairs, perfect masterpieces of the cabinetmaker's art. Behind hung a richly framed painting depicting the famous incident of a mouse freeing a lion from a net, alongside a glass case containing the chart drawn by Miss Bianca for use in the expedition to the Black Castle, and several other trophies of the same nature. There probably wasn't another Moot-hall in the world so dignified, commodious and interesting, or so regularly filled full!

Of the four walnut fauteuils one was for the present Madam Chairwoman, one was for the Treasurer, one was for Bernard as Secretary, and the last for Miss Bianca as P.M.P. As usual, when Bernard led her on there was loud applause, which Miss Bianca as usual acknowledged with a graceful bow before sitting down to be bored.

"Well, here we all are," opened Bernard briskly. "Minutes to be-taken-as-read-any-objection-put-your-hand-up . . ."

Not a hand was raised. ("If only someone *would* object!" thought Miss Bianca. "I'm sure none of them remembers a thing about what was in the last minutes!") She couldn't put her hand up herself because she *did* remember — Item One, permission granted to hold a teen-age dance, Item Two, was there dry rot in the roof? — and couldn't honestly object to either.

"Fine," said Bernard. "I don't think the Treasurer has much to tell us. You most of you seem to be paying your dues all right."

"A hundred per cent," agreed the Treasurer.

"So all we've really got on the Agenda," continued Bernard, "and especially since there *isn't* dry rot after all, is the best way of spending 'em; on which point I believe our esteemed Madam Chairwoman has a jolly good idea about extending Meals-on-Wheels to include hamburgers."

Miss Bianca had often marveled that Bernard, after sharing every single exotic adventure with her, could still appear so concerned with things like hamburgers. ("Remember the mustard!" added Bernard.) "Undoubtedly Bernard's is the better nature," thought Miss Bianca. "Dear me, I wish I didn't feel so bored!"

"Hamburgers!" exclaimed the Madam Chairwoman,

now rising to her feet, also giving Bernard a furious look, for she had meant the hamburgers to come as a surprise. — Miss Bianca sympathized with her, but still felt it rather petty. "Hamburgers for the housebound! — what could be more of a treat for the poor dears? And as our Treasurer assures me that there are ample funds for at least a month's experiment, I suppose the really burning question is — "

She paused dramatically.

"Whether they don't get enough mince as it is?" suggested Bernard — suddenly struck by one of his sensible thoughts.

"Not at all," snapped the Chairwoman, this time without even looking at him. "It's *onions or not?*"

Immediately quite a hubbub arose from the benches, as one mouse after another jumped up to argue pro or con — some declaring a hamburger without onions to be little more than a whited sepulchre, others pointing out how they'd make all the rest of the food smell, others again relating personal anecdotes of a granddad who couldn't abide onions or a grandmother who practically lived on them. It was all quite exciting in its way — but how *parochial,* thought Miss Bianca! When the whole question was referred to a Committee, and the next item on the Agenda turned out to be merely the decorations for the teen-age dance, she felt quite justified in letting her thoughts roam to the Orient . . .

Where a page boy was sent to the elephant lines because his tears spoiled a Ranee's sherbet . . .

Where an elephant perhaps but awaited the order to trample that page boy to smithereens!

3

For Miss Bianca, adjuring Bernard to forget Ali, had not intended the plight of the Ranee's unfortunate protégé to be forgotten too. It was indeed the sort of thing Miss Bianca couldn't possibly forget. To do Bernard justice, if he'd had Miss Bianca's imagination he couldn't have either, but then Bernard had so little imagination at all, the only person he could imagine in distress without actually seeing it was Miss Bianca herself. While she was missing for a whole week in the Diamond Castle Bernard imagined so feverishly, he wore quite a track tramping up and down a new wall-to-wall stamp-paper carpet. At the same time this made him uncommonly useful in an emergency, because he never suffered from nerves beforehand.

"If only Ali hadn't proved such a broken reed!" now reflected Miss Bianca — quite indifferent, (the teen-age dance rearing its head again), as to whether paper lanterns would catch fire and the fire brigade have to be called out. "He presented so obvious a channel of communication! — for his Ambassador has certainly too many weightier matters on his mind to be bothered."

Miss Bianca naturally knew all about not bothering Ambassadors. Sometimes when the Boy's father wasn't to

33

be bothered, even the Boy's mother tiptoed, and once put off a whole garden-party.

"And I've met no others of his suite at all!" thought Miss Bianca. "So who can I possibly contact, visiting the Orient?"

At which moment it suddenly occurred to her that widely traveled as she was, she had never visited the Orient herself . . .

"As for refreshments," the Chairwoman was saying firmly, "the teen-agers must provide them themselves. — Don't you agree, Madam President?"

"Yes, of course; certainly!" said Miss Bianca, returning to the Agenda with a start. "I agree with Madam Chairwoman entirely!"

The Chairwoman looked pleased. She was really an excellent mouse in her way — at least fifteen sons bred up to take responsible positions in the retail trade, and about the same number of daughters either respectably married or teaching school. Grandchildren innumerable came to tea each Sunday after afternoon Sunday school, and most sang in the choir. She was still pleased to have the famous Miss Bianca's approval!

"And you yourself, Miss Bianca, will I hope present the prize for the best couple in the Viennese waltz?" she said eagerly. "I won't inflict the cha-cha on you!"

"I'm so sorry," murmured Miss Bianca. "There's nothing I should have enjoyed more than to present prizes for both the waltz *and* (if requested) the cha-cha; only unfortunately I shall be abroad."

4

"Whatever did you mean by that?" asked Bernard, as he and Miss Bianca stood again at the Pagoda gate. (He always saw her home.)

"Exactly what I said," replied Miss Bianca. "I just feel like taking a little holiday abroad. It seems such an opportunity, with the Boy off to summer camp!"

"Whereabouts abroad?" asked Bernard suspiciously.

"Actually the Orient," said Miss Bianca.

There was a slight pause while Bernard walked in through the gate and pulled up a weed from the nearest flower-bed. — In fact Miss Bianca weeded so carefully herself, what he pulled up wasn't a weed at all, but a pansy resting, and he recognized the error almost at once, but he'd apologized to enough vegetable life already in the conservatory that morning, and wasn't going to start again. He just chucked the pansy-root slap-bang into the middle of Miss Bianca's even more carefully weeded lawn, careless of how untidy it looked.

"I might have known!" groaned Bernard. "I suppose it's that wretched page boy!"

"Wretched indeed!" agreed Miss Bianca — which wasn't quite what Bernard meant. "What heart could fail to be touched by such a pathetic tale?"

"Well, let's say an elephant's," rejoined Bernard grimly. "Oh, Miss Bianca, do pray consider the *size* of an elephant, before you consider tackling one! Haven't you ever heard that even the most ferocious and quite large beasts in the jungle — I dare say hundred-pounders — are afraid of elephants?"

"And have *you* never heard," countered Miss Bianca sweetly, "that *elephants* are afraid of *mice*?"

"I have, and I don't believe it," snapped Bernard. "In my opinion it's just an old wives' tale. — Speaking of which," he added, more moderately, "you do I hope realize that a tale, a word you used yourself first, is probably what the whole thing is, when all you have to go on is the unreliable word of a conceited reptile who probably lifted the whole idea from a movie he saw just to make himself more interesting when he actually caught cold in just some perfectly commonplace way like leaving his galoshes off?"

"I trust you may be right," smiled Miss Bianca. "Nothing would give me greater happiness, than to discover your diagnosis, as it well may prove, perfectly correct. But dear me," she continued lightly — hoping to stop Bernard looking so desperate by suggesting that all she had in mind was a little air travel — "how long it is since I've *flown!* Not since I flew to Norway! And how delightfully swift and commodious airplanes are, compared with dust-carts and narrow-gauge railways!" (Miss Bianca, in the course of prisoner-rescuing, had endured both these uncomfortable modes of transport, so she knew what she was talking about.) "Moreover an airplane with an Ambassador in it will doubtless be the swiftest and most commodious type of all!"

"I see you've got it all taped," said Bernard.

"Well, naturally," said Miss Bianca. "You don't suppose I could keep my mind fixed on hamburgers — or even teen-age dances — for a whole hour? My dear Bernard, I do most sincerely thank you for your warning; and as I say, I only hope you're right; but really the whole point is that I *need* a holiday — and the call of the Orient, combined with air travel, is simply irresistible! Peacocks!" exclaimed Miss Bianca enthusiastically. "To observe peacocks in their native haunts, how charming! Possibly I may even stroke a peacock in its native haunt!" (Actually now that she'd thought of it, the idea really attracted her.) "In fact, as the British poet Rudyard Kipling so well remarked," quoted Miss Bianca (at the same time correcting his grammar), " *'If you've heard the East a-calling, you will never heed aught else!'* "

"Then I suppose they'll have to get the Treasurer to judge the cha-cha," said Bernard gloomily. "If it wasn't you, it was going to be me. When do we start?"

5

Miss Bianca made no attempt to dissuade him from accompanying her. She felt Bernard was growing too parochially minded altogether, so that a change would do him good. She therefore simply thanked him very much, and adjured him to be ready, with hand-luggage only, the following night.

"Since by a most fortunate chance," explained Miss Bianca, "the takeoff is scheduled for eleven P.M.; under cover of darkness we may slip aboard quite easily. — As to how we *get* to the airport," she added, (knowing perfectly well what Bernard was going to say next), "that's easy too: in the Ambassador's, I mean *our* Ambassador's car. He intends to drive to see his colleague off, and with his usual thoughtfulness *doesn't* intend, at that hour of night, to take a chauffeur. We shall have the back part entirely to ourselves."

POEM BY MISS BIANCA
WRITTEN BEFORE GOING TO BED

O Orient! O magic sound!
O magic name! O magic ground!
Where peacocks and Ranees abound
    In colorful profusion!
Or so th'Arabian Nights relate,
And even at this later date
Not I, for one, anticipate
    The pangs of disillusion!

M. B.

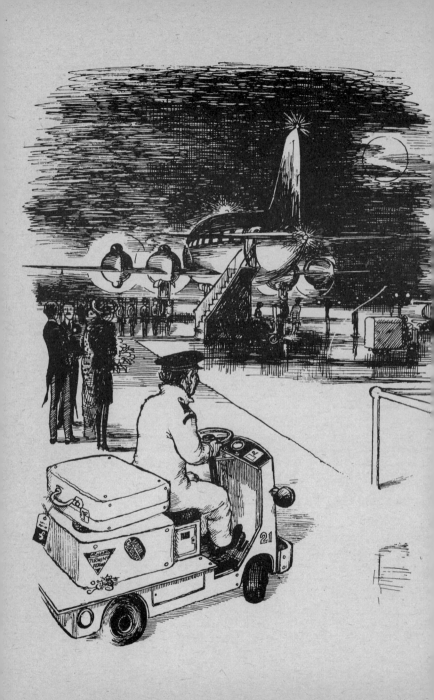

5. To the Orient!

ALL WENT ACCORDING to plan. The Ambassador, his eyes fixed on the road, never gave so much as a glance behind him into the back part of the Ambassadorial car: Bernard and Miss Bianca, though they prudently sat on the floor, could have sat on the seat without being noticed! No one noticed them either as they ran between the boots of a sleepy Guard of Honor and then up the gangway into the plane itself. All present were too preoccupied by such various duties as exchanging diplomatic compliments (the two Ambassadors), keeping awake (the Guard of Honor), and getting airborne on time (the Captain of the aircraft.) If Bernard and Miss Bianca had been the size of poodles, they probably wouldn't have been noticed.

Miss Bianca carried an elegant little overnight bag made of snail-tortoiseshell lined with spider-silk, containing such necessities as a fan, a light chiffon scarf and a flask of eau-de-cologne. Bernard's galoshes and a packet of cough-lozenges — for he had taken warning from Ali's sneezes — were tied up in a spotted handkerchief. Miss Bianca had often urged him to buy a proper brief-case, as more befitting his position as Secretary to the

M.P.A.S., but Bernard was absolutely devoted to his spotted handkerchief ever since Miss Bianca once jumped down into it as into a safety-net, and so probably saved her neck, in the Black Castle. Though touched to see it still in use, the latter was nonetheless glad they hadn't to take provisions, because Bernard's spotted handkerchief with a few sardine-tails sticking out would really have looked quite disreputable! — Bernard had seen her point in a way, and suggested taking something more refined and less oily, like toast crumbs; as he pointed out, cough lozenges were more medicine than grub. But Miss Bianca wouldn't hear even of toast crumbs: having often flown before, she knew that in every passenger plane there is a beautiful young lady dispensing delicious food, sound advice, light literature, general information, and anything else needed. These models of female perfection are called Air Hostesses; and it was under the protection of an Air Hostess that Miss Bianca intended she and Bernard should travel. Miss Bianca, besides all her other qualities, had the top executive's gift of delegating responsibility whenever possible.

Thus no sooner was the plane airborne than the Hostess, taking off her cap before the mirror in her own private cubicle, beheld two mice seated on the shelf underneath, each wearing a label inscribed GIFT TO THE RANEE.

The labels themselves were visiting cards which Miss Bianca had thoughtfully borrowed from the Ambassador. Hers was attached to her silver chain, Bernard's just tied round his neck with a bootlace.

"Good gracious me!" exclaimed the Air Hostess. (She didn't scream, as some ladies do at the sight of mice. Air Hostesses never scream. Even at the sight of baboons loose in the luggage rack an Air Hostess remains calm.) "Good gracious me!" repeated the Air Hostess, as she finished reading. "How did you get out of your cage? — Or traveling compartment," she added, meeting Miss Bianca's slightly reproving eye. (Air Hostesses are noted for their sensitivity and tact.) "Obviously you are V.I.P.'s indeed," she continued, "but what on earth am I to do with you?"

Since they weren't on earth, but in the air, Miss Bianca just sat back and again delegated responsibility. Bernard, who already admired the Air Hostess extremely, with equal confidence sat back and smoothed his whiskers. (Bernard's whiskers haven't so far been done justice to: though short, they were remarkably strong.)

"At any rate I must declare you to the Captain!" decided the Air Hostess.

So she carried Bernard and Miss Bianca off on a soap-dish to the Captain's cabin.

"Presents for the Ranee?" said the Captain. "Why, we must have a hundredweight of stuff for her already! Just see they go with the rest, Miss Fitzpatrick — and you might drop a word to the passengers about what fun monsoons are . . ."

Thus Bernard and Miss Bianca traveled airborne to the Orient in the most comfortable conditions imaginable. Miss Bianca slept on the Hostess's own cushion,

Bernard in her box of Kleenex. Their meals were scrumptious — green salad, coffee cake, and three kinds of cheese. In fact they were quite sorry, at least Bernard was, when the time came to disembark; in fact Bernard was so busy saying good-bye to the Hostess, it was left to Miss Bianca to appreciate the skill with which the Captain made a perfect three-point landing on an airstrip scarcely wider than his plane's wingspan.

"How hazardous, yet how elegant!" thought Miss Bianca — for scarcely two furlongs beyond where the propellers stopped whirling rose the blank wall of a marble palace — the very last sort of thing an aircraft would want to overrun into! Actually this happened to be the only level area in the whole of the mountainy Republic the Oriental Ambassador represented, and actually the strip was already being widened: as she paused on the gangway Miss Bianca observed the enormous shape of an elephant trampling smooth an equal breadth adjoining . . .

"My first elephant!" breathed Miss Bianca rapturously. In the evening light its shadow stretched for yards and yards — to a mouse it was like contemplating one's first Alp! "Let me imprint the image on my memory forever," thought Miss Bianca, "so that I may one day write a poem — nay, an epic! — on the subject!"

She couldn't linger imprinting, however, because at that moment the Air Hostess, with Bernard in one hand already, picked her up in the other. On the airstrip two cars awaited: the Ambassador, followed by his suite, immediately got into the first and it immediately drove off, while the second was as immediately loaded with bales and parcels all addressed to Her Highness the Ranee, and of course Bernard and Miss Bianca, with their labels round their necks, were put in too. But theirs didn't follow the Ambassador's car, for while he was bound to make his report in the Capital hundreds of miles off, the car bearing gifts for the Ranee had but to circle her palace's marble walls to the entrance on the other side. The Capital and the Palace were worlds apart indeed!

They were also worlds apart *mechanically*. While the Ambassador's car rolled smoothly and rapidly away, that containing Bernard and Miss Bianca ran out of petrol at once. — Its chauffeur, an empty can in hand, strolled back to beg from the aircraft: Miss Bianca, to whom all inefficiency was anathema, shifted impatiently on whatever it was she was sitting on. It wasn't at all comfortable — thin and crackly at one end, bumpy at the other; on closer inspection, it turned out to be a packet of mustard-and-cress . . .

A point Miss Bianca had often before noticed about air travel was that however swiftly one traveled *in* the air, there were absolutely no places like air terminals for general hanging about. As the discussion between the chauffeur and the captain of the aircraft opened, continued, and looked likely to continue, Miss Bianca preferred action of any kind to bored passivity. — A paper packet of mustard-and-cress weighed scarcely heavier than her overnight bag; while Bernard was still straining for a last glimpse of the Hostess, out ran Miss Bianca, pulling the packet after her, and with nimble feet sowed its contents just in front of the propellers and was back in the car long ere the necessary petrol was being poured into its tank.

Then they were off at last and at last achieved the short distance to a gateway second in marble beauty only to the Taj Mahal.

2

"One bale of sables," checked the chauffeur with the doorkeeper, "two of silver fox, one ermine bedspread ready-made-up, also a couple of mice — though where *they've* got to I don't know!"

Actually Bernard and Miss Bianca were inside already with their labels off. The latter was so used to having the *entrée* everywhere, she easily ignored even so magnificent a specimen of a doorkeeper as the Ranee's (almost seven feet high, in scarlet with gold epaulettes and a scarlet-and-gold turban). It was Bernard who said shouldn't they tip him; Miss Bianca ignored the suggestion too and walked straight in — Bernard naturally following — and while the baggage was still unloading both had gained the entrance-hall.

"Bless my whiskers!" marveled Bernard.

The hall was indeed quite spectacular. Its walls were faced with pale pink marble, and the twelve pillars supporting a dome above a fish-pool alternately of jasper and porphyry. The pool itself was tiled with lapis lazuli, against which the scales of a few fat lolling carp gleamed topaz-bright. Miss Bianca was struck to admiration herself; even though she felt the whole décor rather too technicolor to be in perfectly good taste, standards of taste varied, thought Miss Bianca, from clime to clime — and hadn't she expected the Orient to be colorful?

Bernard for his part experienced chiefly a sort of overcomeness, as after eating too many marshmallows, but bravely tried not to show it.

"Where do we go from here?" he asked — as if "here" was just a familiar bus stop, or suburban railway station, instead of being all over pink marble. "I mean, what do we do next?"

"Present ourselves to the Ranee, of course," said Miss Bianca briskly. "But first we should be properly dressed!"

Extracting the chiffon scarf from her overnight bag, she rapidly tied it over her nose and in a bow behind.

"As a yashmak," she explained, to the goggling Bernard. "A yashmak, or veil, such as is worn by all ladies in the Orient. I hope you find it becoming?"

"No," said Bernard. "I'm sorry, but I don't, Miss Bianca. I can't see your whiskers."

"'Tis still ever wiser to conform to custom," said Miss Bianca. "*You* must wear a turban!"

With equal swiftness and decision she seized Bernard's spotted handkerchief and wound it round his ears.

— It must be acknowledged that whereas Miss Bianca

in a yashmak looked quite fascinating, Bernard in a turban looked rather silly. Peering at his reflection in the pool, he felt he'd never looked sillier, even when disguised as a member of the M.P.A.S. Ladies' Guild. Still brave Bernard did not flinch; and it is even braver to be brave while looking silly than to be brave while looking not.

"Lead on!" said Bernard gamely.

Miss Bianca did so. Besides being used to having the *entrée,* she was so used to being in places like palaces and courts and embassies and so on, she had little difficulty in guiding their steps through corridors of ever-increasing splendor — first plain marble, then marble inlaid with scraps of looking-glass, then marble inlaid with topaz — until through an arch inlaid with turquoise they reached the Ranee's private apartment. Here the walls were inlaid with jade; underfoot, for what seemed like miles, stretched a wonderful silk carpet woven all round the border with a pattern of pomegranates and in the middle with a great peacock. Beyond, upon a dais, glittered a low divan heaped with cushions covered in silver brocade. Somehow suspended before it a row of jewel-like hummingbirds, though stuffed, appeared to quiver in the air, their tiny claws upholding a panel of finest gauze as a kindly preventive against anyone being blinded by the Ranee's beauty as there she sat on her silver brocade cushions surrounded by a dozen or so ladies sitting lower down.

"My whiskers!" muttered Bernard again.

Miss Bianca, though silently, agreed with him. The Ranee was in fact the most beautiful person either of them had ever beheld. — Most Ambassadors' wives, of whom Miss Bianca had seen scores, are good-looking; the Boy's mother was quite lovely; but not one could hold a candle to the Ranee. Her face was a perfect oval, her complexion ivory lightly flushed with rose; beneath eyebrows black and graceful as a swallow's wings, lashes even longer than Miss Bianca's shaded a pair of glorious dark eyes. As for her mouth, it was so rose-like in color and petal-shapeliness, one almost imagined it a rose indeed, only with for heart a glimpse of pearl.

Besides being so beautiful, she was also exquisitely dressed. Over trousers of some light Oriental gauze — dark blue, embroidered with sapphires — she wore by way of contrast a white silk tunic barely touched with silver. Her jewels were equally well-chosen and becoming: a diamond necklace fastened with a sapphire clasp, about twenty-four diamond bracelets, and in her wonderful dark hair six or seven diamond stars.

"*She* isn't wearing a veil," muttered Bernard.

"Because we are in her private apartments," murmured Miss Bianca, swiftly removing her own yashmak, and indeed feeling happier as her whiskers sprang out again. "But do you keep your turban on, Bernard; it looks more respectful."

At which moment, the Ranee yawned. All the ladies sitting round her looked nervous. One hastily offered a little gold dish of crystallized violets, another a little gold dish of pistachio nuts. The Ranee nibbled a nibble from each with her pearly teeth, then yawned again.

"Now is our time!" whispered Miss Bianca. "Evidently conversation flags; I don't think we shall be unwelcome!"

Bernard following, she advanced boldly over the peacock-carpet to within a foot of the cushion-throne. There she halted and bowed, while Bernard took three paces forward, then one back, and pulled his whiskers.

There was indeed no doubt of their welcome!

"Good gracious!" exclaimed the Ranee delightedly. "Fill someone's mouth with gold! See, just as I'm about to expire from boredom, someone's found me two nice new pets!"

3

It was a moment that called for all Miss Bianca's diplomacy, self-forgetfulness in a good cause, general sharp-wittedness and *savoir-faire*. Both she and Bernard strongly objected to being called pets — Miss Bianca could positively feel Bernard beginning to bristle — but at the same time she immediately perceived that to introduce herself as Perpetual Madam President of the M.P.A.S. would cut no ice with the Ranee. In the latter's glorious dark eyes Miss Bianca instantly and accurately read merely a desire to be entertained before she expired of boredom, and absolutely no interest whatever in even such things as Meals-on-Wheels.

"That is, I suppose they can *do* something?" added the Ranee — already impatient! "They can dance or sing or something?"

"You can jolly well suppose again!" muttered Bernard furiously. "The lady I have the honor to escort — "

"Hush!" adjured Miss Bianca. "Is this a time for *amour-propre?* Impersonate a wandering minstrel!"

For her eye had been most fortunately caught by a little bibelot in the shape of a miniature harp standing on a low mother-of-pearl table beside the Ranee's sofa-throne. Miss Bianca instantly ran up and struck a few chords. The strings, though of gold wire, responded sweetly to her touch; even though each pedal was a pearl, and thus dreadfully slippery, she managed to control them. First she played "Greensleeves," then that exquisite mouse minuet "Le Camembert," while Bernard, without knowing it — he'd just rushed up to be at her side —

appeared by his agitated gestures to be turning over invisible music for her. The effect upon the Ranee was instantaneous.

"It's the prettiest thing ever seen!" declared the Ranee.

"The prettiest thing ever seen!" echoed all her ladies.

"I shall take both into my service at once!" decided the Ranee.

"Her Highness will take both into her service at once!" all the ladies told each other.

"Prepare everything mice like to eat, also a suitable cage!" ordered the Ranee.

All the ladies rushed out, leaving Bernard and Miss Bianca alone to amuse Her Highness.

It proved no light task. The Ranee was so enchanted by Miss Bianca's touch in "Le Camembert," she demanded it again and again, until Bernard saw Miss Bianca so fatigued, he had to fan her with his whiskers. This enchanted the Ranee even more ("Prepare a cage of gold!" cried she, to her returning ladies) and Bernard no less than Miss Bianca was quite exhausted before the Ranee remembered three hundred guests to dinner.

"But you shall entertain me again tomorrow!" she promised. "Tomorrow, you shall entertain me all day long!"

4

The golden cage produced by the Ranee's ladies was as commodious as splendid, having once housed a pair of cockatoos. (A long scarlet tail-feather, still dangling between the bars, added further splendor.) Bernard moved into a little upstairs flat, originally a bird-seed pan, while Miss Bianca took the ground floor. The eager ladies supplied bedding out of their own pockets — that is, out of their own pocket-handkerchieves — and two of the youngest and prettiest brought in addition to cream cheese and crystallized violets a scent-spray containing attar of roses to spray all about and make it smell nice.

"Well!" said Bernard, as soon as they were gone. "I

55

can't say I much liked being taken for a wandering minstrel, but these quarters are absolutely A-one!"

"Nothing could be more comfortable," agreed Miss Bianca. "And really, my dear Bernard, I'd no idea you had such a talent for amateur dramatics!"

This was particularly tactful, as making him feel rather pleased with himself, instead of that he'd made rather an ass of himself. But indeed Bernard seemed in an unexpectedly good mood altogether. For one thing, he didn't even bristle about the cage being a cage — as a rule, being in anything like a cage made Bernard bristle at once! — and even suggested thinking up a name for it, like the Porcelain Pagoda.

"Like 'Home Sweet Home,'" offered Bernard.

"Why not 'Chez Cockatoo'?" smiled Miss Bianca. "Now I can't keep my eyes open a moment longer!" she added. " 'Tis high time to say good-night!"

Bernard of course made for his upstairs flat at once. — On its threshold he paused.

"I say, Miss Bianca!" he called down.

"Well?" yawned Miss Bianca, already slipping between sweet-scented handkerchief-sheets.

"Possibly you didn't notice," said Bernard, "but I did: in the whole of the Ranee's court there wasn't a single page boy to be seen! She doesn't *have* page boys! Good-night, Miss Bianca."

6. At the Court of the Ranee

"DEAR ME!" THOUGHT Miss Bianca, as soon as she woke next morning. "What Bernard says is correct: there *weren't* any pages!"

Sitting up and considering, she distinctly remembered the Ranee's constant crunching of nuts or crystallized violets during the pianissimo parts of "Le Camembert," also that each little golden dish was offered by one of her ladies. On the other hand, if there hadn't been any page boys, there hadn't been any sherbet either.

"Perhaps 'tis only sherbet the pages serve?" meditated Miss Bianca. "By some Oriental custom? Today let me watch carefully!"

2

She had ample opportunity to do so, since the Ranee was so delighted with her new pets, she kept them beside her at every waking hour. (It may be said at once, in case anyone besides Bernard is worried over Miss Bianca becoming thoroughly exhausted, that this crush didn't last long; quite soon Miss Bianca was summoned to the harp only at evening.) During that first next day, however, she was constantly at the throne-side; and had ample opportunity to observe the sherbet-service that went on all morning each hour on the hour — but performed strictly by Her Highness's ladies. Cups of coffee also appeared, and trays of Turkish Delight — the Ranee was always either sipping or nibbling something — but never a sign of a page boy.

"Strange!" thought Miss Bianca. "Can it be that the unfortunate orphan described by Ali was Her Highness's single and solitary experiment in that direction, never repeated? Or has Bernard been correct all along, in his suspicions of Ali's utter if imaginative untrustworthiness?"

She honorably relayed these thoughts to Bernard himself. Though naturally pleased, he was too big — just as Miss Bianca was too big *not* to relay them — to say anything like "I told you so," but instead listened sympathetically when she went on to think (aloud) that a few discreet inquiries were still called for.

"Though if you're going to inquire of the Ranee," said Bernard dubiously, "whether she had a youngster sent to the elephant lines just because he sniveled a bit — "

"I agree 'twould be hardly tactful," said Miss Bianca. "I believe I'll ask Willow . . ."

3

Willow was the oldest of the Ranee's ladies: willow-slim indeed, also quivering, like a willow, with sensibility. Striking the harp, Miss Bianca had observed Willow's face through the strings fixed in a look of such sweet, sad rapture, she'd have played for her alone! — But it was also a *sensible* face, and Miss Bianca, ever famous for her swift summing-up of character, at once felt Willow her best source of information. Unluckily, however, there never seemed an opportunity to broach the subject, for the latter, whenever not on duty in the throne-room, had a knack of disappearing. Miss Bianca truly regretted it, though when she learnt the reason, during a talk with the very youngest and prettiest lady (the one who'd sprayed Chez Cockatoo with scent, and whose name was Vanilla), she thought more highly of Willow still.

"Darling Willow takes such care of us all, she never has a *moment*," explained Vanilla. "Some of us come into Her Highness's service so young, and miss our families so, we sometimes cry in bed a little — don't we, Muslin?"

Muslin was the second prettiest of the Ranee's ladies, and the one who'd brought the cream cheese and crystallized violets.

"And then darling Willow comes and holds our hands," continued Vanilla, "and if you want she'll teach you to embroider, or dance, or sing, or even play chess — all sorts of things! — and takes such pains, she never has a spare moment!"

"Good Willow!" reflected Miss Bianca. "Is it not just what one might have expected, from your sensitive, sensible and charming countenance? One can well imagine

59

you never have a spare moment! And am I come to add to your pains and agitate you with my distressing inquiries? — Perhaps I needn't after all," thought Miss Bianca suddenly, "for I certainly don't mind agitating Muslin and Vanilla!"

The three were chatting outside Chez Cockatoo — Muslin and Vanilla having taken it upon themselves always to see Miss Bianca back to bed after a concert.

"And how long have *you* been at the Palace, my dears?" asked Miss Bianca interestedly.

"Oh, ages!" said Vanilla.

"Years and years!" said Muslin.

"So that if within the last *month,*" continued Miss Bianca, "there had been any page boy in the Ranee's service, and if he had been sufficiently unhappy as to cry into her Highness's sherbet, and as a consequence be sent to the elephant lines, you'd remember?"

Both Muslin and Vanilla looked quite horrified!

"How could we? No one's *ever* unhappy in Her Highness's service!" declared Vanilla. "It's a rule — isn't it, Muslin?"

"The first rule," agreed Muslin.

"But one which a lonely little boy might find difficulty in learning?" suggested Miss Bianca.

"Only there never *was* such a boy," declared Vanilla positively. "Can *you* remember any page boy crying into Her Highness's sherbet, Muslin?"

"Never!" shuddered Muslin.

"You're quite certain?" pressed Miss Bianca.

"Quite, quite certain!" declared Muslin and Vanilla with one voice.

"Good gracious," Miss Bianca told herself. "I believe I really *am* going to have a holiday!"

According to Bernard (better pleased than ever at Miss Bianca's fresh report), more than a full week of holidaying lay ahead; for Bernard had taken a look at the Air Hostess's time-sheet — he was afraid she might be overworked — and could confidently affirm that the plane's next takeoff westwards, again with the Ambassador on board, wasn't scheduled before nine days' time.

4

Certainly there was no better place for holidaying than in the Ranee's palace. The way the day went was like this:

First, until the Ranee woke, which was usually late, all was as still and silent and restful as a lily-pool. Of course all the ladies were awake earlier, but moved about on tiptoe, and sipped their coffee, and helped each other arrange their hair and jewels and saris, with no more rustle than the first breath of a dawn breeze. This was a period Miss Bianca particularly enjoyed. Slipping out from Chez Cockatoo to watch, she felt she'd never witnessed anything prettier than Her Highness's ladies tiptoeing about, and arranging each other's saris and jewels and hair, all as 'twere in a silent film!

Then as soon as Her Highness woke up, a silver bell summoned them to Her Highness's private marble bath to lave her in rose-water, and then dry her on swansdown towels, before perfuming her with musk and amber and essence of jasmine. Her own morning coffee was floated to her on a little tray of cedarwood carved in the shape of a lily-pad.

After which exertions the Ranee adjourned to her divan-throne (now spread with an ermine bedspread ready-made-up), to partake of the light refreshments already described until lunchtime, and after lunch went to sleep again, while the ladies adjourned to their swimming pool, where the scene was far livelier. They splashed each other, sometimes even ducked each other, threw gaily colored balls to one another, often shrieking with laughter — for during this period the Ranee was by her own command counted only semi-asleep, and rather enjoyed, since it was her declared aim to make everyone about her happy, sounds of (distant) merriment.

Then when Her Highness had sufficiently roused to take tea, the next two hours were spent in bathing and dressing her afresh before she reascended her throne to be entertained before she died of boredom.

Miss Bianca was truly shocked at the amount of entertainment the Ranee needed to prevent this happening. "To be so rich, and lovely, and yet so bored!" thought Miss Bianca distressfully. "No doubt 'tis a fault of education; but how unfortunate the result! I wonder if I could interest her in Meals-on-Wheels?"

But even Miss Bianca, who always tried to take the best view of human nature, felt probably not. The Ranee's glorious dark eyes lit with some spark of interest only at the sight of jugglers juggling, or acrobats somersaulting, or when Miss Bianca played upon the harp or when one of the numerous court poets recited a poem in praise of her beauty . . .

To Miss Bianca this last phase of each evening's entertainment was by far the most enjoyable. Though the subject matter was necessarily rather monotonous, as a poet herself she was always interested in technique. Poetry written in Oriental, discovered Miss Bianca, had very short lines, with the same few number of syllables in each, and no more than six lines altogether making up a stanza. Miss Bianca quite marveled at a poet's skill in comparing the Ranee to a lotus, a gazelle and the full moon all so to speak in a single breath! — and soon determined to try her hand herself, though upon a different theme.

POEM BY MISS BIANCA
WRITTEN IN ORIENTAL

Bulbuls * in groves
Stretch forth their throats
Mingling with doves'
Musical notes
Sweet to the ears
Of boatmen in boats.

M. B.

As a first attempt it was really excellent — only one syllable too many in the last line. "But how lacking in *heart!*" thought Miss Bianca; and to be true to her own muse, immediately sought inspiration afresh.

POEM BY MISS BIANCA
WRITTEN WITH MORE INSPIRATION

Far, far have we flown, o'er mountains and foam,
O'er deltas and deserts, brave Bernard and I!
Shall we e'er feel again the kiss of the rain
Or watch for the first fall of snow?
Ah, no, I much fear me, ah no!

"But this is perfectly ridiculous!" Miss Bianca admonished herself. "Of course we shall — and Bernard will

* Oriental for nightingale.

be complaining about how his chimney smokes, and I sealing the double windows in my Pagoda!"

So she hastily composed two lines more.

> *Of course we shall! — and well content*
> *Discuss our venture to the Orient!*

M. B.

Bernard liked this second poem very much. The first he frankly admitted he couldn't make tail or whiskers of — especially since bulbuls sounded to him like some sort of peppermint; and even after Miss Bianca had explained, wouldn't boatmen in *boats,* pointed out Bernard, presumably fishing, be too far offshore anyway to hear either doves *or* nightingales? But the second poem, with brave Bernard in it, he liked so much he learnt it off by heart.

Miss Bianca's chief allies at the Ranee's court continued to be Muslin and Vanilla. They were best friends. Muslin was dark, Vanilla fair, but owing to their common expression of sweetness and good nature looked rather alike. They proved indeed the best-natured girls imaginable, and did everything in their power to make Miss Bianca happy.

"Because we've quite fallen in love with you! — haven't we, Muslin?" cooed Vanilla.

"Because we think you're the sweetest and cleverest

little thing we've ever seen — don't we, Vanilla?" cooed Muslin.

If there was something rather schoolgirlish about their devotion, Miss Bianca only smiled. The affectionate pair indeed took as much care of her as possible — Muslin always ready to carry her to bed after an over-long session at the harp, Vanilla, the bolder spirit, always ready to chaperone a run for fresh air on a door-sill. Miss Bianca in turn grew truly fond of the two friends, and truly appreciated their company — especially after Bernard left Chez Cockatoo to take up quarters in the stables.

It wasn't exactly Bernard's fault that he became *persona non grata* — which translated from diplomatic means about as welcome as a gumboil — in the Ranee's throne-room. It just so happened that while Miss Bianca was giving her third or fourth recital on the harp, and while Bernard was pretending to turn over music for her, he sneezed. The air of the throne-room was so thick with scent (and Bernard didn't even smoke), a whiff of musk caught him unawares. Luckless Bernard sneezed and sneezed; the Ranee frowned and frowned; and Miss Bianca thoroughly agreed with her new friends that he had better make himself, at least temporarily, scarce.

"No one would notice him in the stables," said Vanilla kindly. "I believe they're quite full of common brown mice!"

Naturally Bernard disliked being taken for common almost as much as he disliked being taken for a pet or a wandering minstrel, and Miss Bianca sympathized with him; but she couldn't help feeling a change of address sensible. As she pointed out, he could still keep on his flat at Chez Cockatoo and drop in from time to time.

"But what about *you*, Miss Bianca?" argued Bernard. "How can I possibly leave you all alone and unprotected at night?"

"I dare say Muslin and Vanilla will accommodate Chez Cockatoo in their sleeping apartment," smiled Miss Bianca.

"Indeed we will!" cried Muslin and Vanilla. "There's just the proper space between our beds!"

Faced by three females, all of them beauties, Bernard knew he hadn't a chance; and shifted quarters within the hour.

5

Actually Bernard was a great success in the stables. As a rule, when out on expeditions with Miss Bianca, he was so anxious for her safety every minute he could never take an opportunity to enjoy himself even if one offered; but seeing her so obviously cherished and protected he for once felt free to get around a bit, and chummed up with a set of bachelor mice who taught him to play polo.

— The gear was neat, if old-fashioned, pith helmets, and Bernard easily borrowed one, in which he felt far more at home than in a turban. As he for the first time took the field he in fact looked rather dashing, and only wished Miss Bianca there to see.

Those who have never played polo (as of course Bernard hitherto hadn't) cannot conceive with what force the opposing ponies and their riders rush down upon each other. Bernard, clinging to the root of his pony's tail (Number Three), had the breath almost knocked out of his body. Rough words equally beat about his ears as a princely rider reined and checked. — Bernard didn't know what else to do, so he nipped as hard as he could on a shining quarter and found himself carried, with acclaim, through the opposing goal . . .

After so successful a debut Bernard played polo regularly. His team was called the Princely Orchids. He was also put up for, and joined, the Mouse Oriental Polo Club.

So Bernard was having a holiday too — while as for Miss Bianca's own success at court, it was quite spectacular!

7. An Unwelcome Gift, and Worse to Follow

"SEE WHAT the Ranee's given you!" cried Vanilla, opening her handkerchief.

"Look what the Ranee's given you!" echoed Muslin.

Miss Bianca gasped as out tumbled a ruby necklace, two pairs of diamond earrings, and several diamond or emerald rings. (They were actually just what the Ranee had lying about on her dressing-table. Its drawers contained ten times as much in the way of jewelry. Her strongbox contained an opal the size of a peach and pearls bigger than pigeon's eggs.) It was still an immensely valuable gift, and as Vanilla pointed out, more valuable still as a mark of the Ranee's favor.

"I'm really overwhelmed!" said Miss Bianca. — The next moment she was indeed; as Muslin looped the rubies about her neck, Miss Bianca sat down with less than her usual grace. "Let's try twining them round your tail," suggested Vanilla anxiously, "for you really and positively must *wear* them, darling Miss Bianca!" But with her tail wreathed in rubies Miss Bianca was simply anchored. "If you'd let us ever so gently pierce your ears," suggested Muslin, "I'm sure you could wear at least the earrings!" "I'm sorry, but I'm quite sure I couldn't," said Miss Bianca firmly. "Why, I should feel as though I were wearing a *yoke!*" (There was a double meaning in this which neither of the ladies appreciated.) "In fact," said Miss Bianca, "grateful as I am to Her Highness — if necessary I'll make a song about it — such a mass of jewelry is really too much for me to support."

Even if she could have she wouldn't have, because she considered any *mass* of jewelry extremely vulgar. Naturally Miss Bianca couldn't say this to Muslin and Vanilla, who wore every trinket they possessed from the moment they got up.

She saw them look at each other in dismay.

"Dear, darling Miss Bianca," said Vanilla earnestly, "you really and positively must wear at least *part* of the Ranee's gifts about your person, or she'll be quite terribly offended — and not only with *you,* with *us!*"

The last thing Miss Bianca wanted was to get the pair into trouble. — One of the emerald rings, though the stone was superb beyond belief, had for shank but a slim hoop of gold; and after trying it on Miss Bianca found she could wear it round her neck without actual discomfort, much to the relief of her two friends.

"You must still make up that song, Miss Bianca!" warned Muslin.

SONG COMPOSED BY MISS BIANCA
TO EXPLAIN WHY SHE WASN'T WEARING
A RUBY NECKLACE AND DIAMOND EARRINGS
ETC. AS WELL

O'ercome with gratitude I sing,

warbled Miss Bianca to the harp

The humble wearer of Her Highness' em'rald ring!
Rubies and diamonds too? Ah, far too rare
For one who strums so dull an air!
 Rubies are her Highness' lips
 Tra-la-la, and finger tips.
 Diamonds match her sparkling gaze
 Tra-la-la, and witty ways.
 Diamond and ruby-stone
 Are for the Ranee alone!
  Tra-la-la-la-la.

"Well, I must say I think that's rather nice," said the Ranee, "and shows a very becoming modesty. Muslin and

Vanilla, you can just put the rest of my gift back on my dressing-table."

Miss Bianca was rather sorry to hear this, as she'd meant to turn over all the other jewels as a present to her two friends. However Muslin and Vanilla seemed quite delighted by this mark of Her Highness's confidence — and in fact subsequently wore an extra ring apiece, only Her Highness didn't notice.

Such was the way of life in the Ranee's palace!

Miss Bianca sighed. One thing she was determined upon was that when she took the plane for home again, the emerald should be left behind. She still continued to wear it round her neck, however, at least on duty; and was forced to admit, whenever she passed a mirror, that the quarter-inch square of green fire had probably never looked better than against her own soft, silvery fur.

2

Bernard didn't like it at all.

"I'm sorry to say so, Miss Bianca," remarked Bernard, "and I never thought I'd have to say so, but I must say I think you look a bit overdressed."

" 'When in Rome, do as the Romans do,' " quoted Miss Bianca lightly. "And isn't it at least extraordinarily beautiful?"

"I suppose it's beautiful all right," admitted Bernard. "Only you don't look like yourself, Miss Bianca, peeping

out over what however beautiful looks to me like a traffic-
light . . ."

Miss Bianca didn't feel quite like herself herself. She
wasn't used to taking holidays. In fact the whole atmosphere of the Ranee's palace was already beginning to re-
mind her of the atmosphere in the salt mine whither she
and Bernard had once penetrated in the interests of
prisoner-rescuing: the same unnatural beauty and tran-
quillity, the same ease of living . . .

And the same undercurrent of danger . . .

3

Evidently there were some parts of Ali's tale he hadn't
made up.

Once, as a court poet stumbled over a rhyme —

"I suppose you know," said the Ranee coldly, "where
the elephant lines are?"

"No, your Highness; that is, yes, your Highness,"
cringed the poor poet, turning pale.

"And you know what class of persons are sent there?"
continued the Ranee, selecting a crystallized violet.

"Those who have the misfortune — however unwittingly — to offend your Highness," gasped the poet.

"And you know what happens to them at the next full
moon?" continued the Ranee — crunching the violet be-

tween her beautiful little sharp teeth. "If you don't, ask my Head Pastry Cook! Only of course you can't; good Hathi trampled him to puff-pastry a fortnight ago. So you'd better," concluded the Ranee, "think quickly of a more suitable rhyme to 'lily' than '*silly*' . . ."

Not unnaturally, the poet was struck dumb. But Miss Bianca, however horrified, kept her wits.

" '*Chilly*,' " supplied Miss Bianca, in a rapid undertone. " '*Something-something *lily*,' then something-something — never mind about the six syllables! — such as 'more fair and awe-inspiring still / because so calm and *chilly*.' "

"Now that's what I call really clever!" exclaimed the volatile Ranee, as the poet hastily repeated Miss Bianca's improvisation. " 'Fair and awe-inspiring' is just how I *feel*! Fill his mouth with gold!"

The grateful poet attempted to pass at least one of the gold pieces on to Miss Bianca, but she turned away shuddering; and under cover of the general excitement found an opportunity to address Willow at last.

"Can it really be," murmured Miss Bianca, "that so dreadful a sentence would indeed have been carried out?"

"Hush!" murmured back Willow. "Dear little person, try not to think of such things — as I try never to let my girls think of them!"

"No whispering!" snapped the Ranee — her pretty ears evidently as sharp as her pretty teeth. "Don't you know whispering's *very bad manners?*"

4

"This is a dangerous place indeed," thought Miss Bianca, "and thank goodness Bernard has the stables to sneeze in! — I wonder" she thought suddenly, "what happened to the cockatoos?"

For a mouse to be haunted by the ghost of a cockatoo was obviously quite ridiculous. Miss Bianca, in bed that night, wasn't precisely haunted — that is, she didn't see cockatoo shapes or hear cockatoo voices, but she couldn't help continuing to wonder what had become of them. She knew cockatoos to be exceptionally long-lived birds; the Ambassadress, the Boy's mother, cherished a pink-and-white specimen said to be the same age as the Boy — and he nearly ten. The sleek scarlet feather still dangling from a golden wire suggested birds quite in the prime of life . . .

The answer she got from Vanilla next morning did nothing to make her feel happier.

"Why, they were strangled!" said Vanilla, rather lightly. "The night someone brought them out for Her Highness's entertainment and the big one fluttered straight into her face!"

"Her Highness fainted three times running and had to be revived with pearls dissolved in wine!" said Muslin.

"When if there's anything Her Highness dislikes it's waste of pearls," added Vanilla. "But I do assure you, darling Miss Bianca, the cage was so thoroughly cleaned out afterwards, you're in no slightest danger of catching psittacosis!"

Miss Bianca was glad to hear it. It still pained her to think of the fate of her ex-so-to-speak-landlords; with her usual delicacy, she particularly regretted having christened her inherited residence so light-heartedly. "Chez Cockatoo" suggested a cottage *orné,* or small pleasure house, not the home of martyrs to a Ranee's weak nerves and sense of economy. "For no doubt 'twas but fright made the poor bird flap in so unfortunate a direction!" thought Miss Bianca. "How small the offense to bring so great a punishment!"

But that too was the way of life at the Ranee's court. Miss Bianca began to feel very lonely in it. Muslin and Vanilla, however devoted, she couldn't help regarding rather in the light of pets, while with Willow, whom she'd hoped to make a friend, she furthered no more acquaintance, since Willow (no doubt because her hands were so full) seemed to have been excused attendance in the throne-room altogether. — Plucking the harp strings in a pianissimo passage of "Le Camembert," Miss Bianca looked in vain for any other equally sensitive and appreciative face. The Ranee munched pistachio nuts and crystallized violets: so, encouraged by her example, did all the other ladies; and what annoyed Miss Bianca most of all, not one even noticed if in her natural irritation she struck a false chord . . .

In short a holiday was a holiday but Miss Bianca couldn't wait to board a westbound plane. She began to count the days; and was thus all the more dismayed when Bernard, when there were only two left to go, suddenly proposed staying on a bit longer.

5

It was a measure of his esteem for Miss Bianca that despite his new obsession Bernard dropped in at Chez Cockatoo most mornings. He could never stay long, because the round trip from the stables and back took about seven hours, but unless the Princely Orchids actually had a match, not just a practice, in the afternoon, Bernard made it.

"Well, they beat 'em!" panted Bernard, mopping his brow with his spotted handkerchief (now returned to its natural uses). "Five goals to one, no less!"

"Who whom?" inquired Miss Bianca politely.

"The Princely Lotuses," explained Bernard. "Yesterday, they licked the Princely Tiger-lilies into a cocked hat! After us Orchids they're the hottest bet in the Tournament — and now we'll meet 'em in the Finals next Thursday. My word, what a game that's going to be!"

Miss Bianca paused, mentally counting the days again.

"When I'm sure you'll play a distinguished part," said she. "That is, if available. Next Thursday, did you say? By next Thursday, shouldn't we already have boarded the Ambassador's westward-bound plane — next Monday?"

"Oh, he's always flipping back and forth," said Bernard carelessly. "We'll just catch the next flight out."

Once more Miss Bianca paused. It may be remembered that she'd hoped a visit to the Orient would broaden Bernard's mind. She hadn't thought of polo as particularly mind-broadening — in fact she hadn't thought of polo at all — but as Bernard went on to remark that he'd sooner be minced to cat-meat than let the team down, and as she recalled that nothing could induce him to play bowls for the M.P.A.S. Bowling Club if he had the Treasurer's accounts to check, she perceived his mind broadened indeed, if in an unexpected direction.

"Anyway you're quite happy here, aren't you, Miss Bianca?" said Bernard. "You don't *mind* staying a few days longer?"

How could Miss Bianca bear to see his loyal whiskers droop in disappointment? She couldn't.

"Quite!" affirmed Miss Bianca.

Thus it happened that she was still at hand to witness the next, ominous full moon rise over the elephant lines . . .

8. Worse Still!

IN THE INTERIM Miss Bianca, however distastefully, continued to wear an emerald worth a prince's ransom round her neck, both rubbing her fur and weighing on her spirits; for there is nothing more repugnant to a delicate nature than to have to take a present from someone one dislikes, and by this time Miss Bianca disliked the Ranee almost as much as she'd disliked the jailers in the Black Castle: somehow the Ranee's ravishing beauty made her careless cruelty all the more repellent. Miss Bianca wore the jewel with increasing repugnance; on the other hand, if she hadn't been wearing it, probably the peacock would have simply ignored her . . .

It may also be remembered that to stroke a peacock in its native haunts was something Miss Bianca really wanted to do, and she had been greatly disappointed to find the one woven into the throne-room carpet the single specimen handy. It was upon the terrace outside that the real live peacocks strutted, and hitherto Miss Bianca had been too fully occupied indoors to attempt acquaintance with them. A day or so after her conversation with Bernard, however, she found an opportunity to slip out during the Ranee's afternoon slumbers, and there not a yard distant stood the most magnificent peacock imaginable, just as though waiting by appointment!

"Good day," said Miss Bianca, with a graceful bow.

After a moment's hesitation, the peacock bowed back. (It was during this moment that he observed the emerald glittering round her neck and recognized it as a quite extraordinary badge of court favor. On a peacock proud as a peacock it acted as a sort of snobbish charm.)

"My salaams," said the peacock, bowing back.

His iridescent throat actually brushed the marble pavement. — It was too tempting altogether! Miss Bianca, who had naturally intended to wait until their acquaintance ripened, couldn't resist the opportunity.

"Would you mind if I stroked you?" asked Miss Bianca impulsively. " 'Twill fulfill one of my dearest dreams," she added, "which I had begun to believe but a dream indeed!"

"Not at all," said the peacock graciously. (Besides being proud as a peacock he was vain as a peacock.) "A very natural ambition!"

Delicately Miss Bianca laid her hand on the short blue-green-purple plumage. Delicately stroking, she felt almost an electric shock, such as any contact with sheer beauty always produces in the aesthetically sensitive. Miss Bianca was both aesthetic and sensitive to a high degree — as the peacock at once appreciated. To do him justice, he appreciated it almost as much as he did her jewelry.

"I dare say you'd care to see me unfurl?" he suggested.

"If it's not too much trouble!" begged Miss Bianca.

"Well, I don't usually at this hour," said the peacock, "but to please a lady of such obvious taste and discrimination as yourself, here goes! — You'll get a better view if you stand back a bit."

Upon which, and as Miss Bianca took his advice, slowly and majestically he raised the great multicolored fan that was his tail. To Miss Bianca, at ground level, it looked like the Aurora Borealis dyed in rainbows . . .

"Superb!" murmured she. "Quite, quite superb!"

"I thought you'd enjoy it," said the peacock. "With more breeze, I could have shown you something really spectacular. 'The painted sail of a storm-tossed galleon,' " he added musingly, "to quote another of my admirers who was a poet . . ."

"I myself have ventured into verse," confessed Miss Bianca.

"One perceived immediately that you were mistress of every elegant and ladylike accomplishment," returned the peacock courteously.

"Published," said Miss Bianca.

"Really?" said the peacock, looking at once both surprised and impressed. (He had taken Miss Bianca for a gifted amateur.) "Actually published?"

"My last slim volume," recalled Miss Bianca, "went into three editions; and I believe is actually reprinting."

"Success indeed!" said the peacock. "And not only success, fame! — I suppose you couldn't toss off a little impromptu? My wife likes to preserve such things in her Memory Book."

Miss Bianca rose to the challenge with all an expert's, and artist's, pleasure. (Fortunately she'd thought of the Aurora Borealis already.) After but a moment's reflection to get the metre right —

"Why, certainly!" said Miss Bianca,

> The Northern Lights, th' Aurora Borealis,
> Are far less splendid-colored than your tail is.

"Charming!" declared the peacock, furling again. "My wife *will* be pleased! — If you care to stroke my tail-feathers as well, I haven't the least objection."

Though the big peacock-eyes were now hidden under brown silky fronds, Miss Bianca as she accepted the offer felt the beauty-thrill again. It made her whole journey to the Orient worthwhile! As they began to stroll on to-

gether, chatting of poetry and the charms of Nature, Miss
Bianca was really enjoying herself. Miss Bianca quoted
a few lines of Keats's "Ode to a Nightingale," the peacock
a whole verse of Hafiz's parallel "Ode to a Bulbul." On
the cultural plane they grew positively intimate — and
even on a lower: turning back from the terrace's limit,
the peacock quite avuncularly warned Miss Bianca that
she shouldn't stray too far outside the palace with such
a precious jewel about her neck, in case of thieves.

"Surely *you* shouldn't stray too far either?" said Miss
Bianca lightly, "trailing a whole tailful of gems more
precious still!"

She spoke really by way of compliment: to her surprise, the peacock looked seriously worried.

"It *is* a great responsibility," he acknowledged. "You
wouldn't believe how constantly on the alert I have to be,
not to get it trodden on; for then if I make the least un-
considered movement — my eye-feathers are particularly
lightly attached — out comes a whole sheaf to be stolen
away and made into fans!"

This was something Miss Bianca hadn't thought of.
She was shocked.

"What vandalism!" she exclaimed feelingly. "I hope
such barbarous attempts don't occur often?"

"Well, not so often since Her Highness got rid of that
sniveling little page boy," said the peacock grimly.

9. Revelations

Miss Bianca's whiskers quivered. She paused. (O delightful promenade, so harshly interrupted!)

"A page boy?" she repeated. "Why, Her Highness has never had a page boy!"

"Dear me," remarked the peacock. "I wonder who told you that?"

"Why, two of her ladies," rejoined Miss Bianca. "By name Muslin and Vanilla."

"*That* pair of noodles!" said the peacock, with an indulgent smile. "Very nice, pretty girls I'm sure — but really with no more memory, let alone observation, than a couple of grasshoppers. They haven't a clue as to what goes on in the Palace! — No doubt it's in part due to Madam Willow's training," he added, "and one can appreciate her motive: our beloved Ranee is so insistent on having only happy faces about her, to learn neither to observe nor remember is probably the first lesson — as the second is to say whatever she, or indeed anyone else, wants to hear. The poet Omar, now — "

"Pray excuse me," said Miss Bianca. "Never has a conversation been more enjoyable; but just at the moment I have rather urgent business indoors."

With which, after a hurried but still graceful bow, she turned and ran as quickly as she could to find Muslin and Vanilla.

2

Her two friends were in the big marble swimming pool, also fortunately alone there. (All the other ladies had suddenly adopted a craze for mah-jongg.) As soon as they saw Miss Bianca approach, they called to her to come and join them.

"Come in, Miss Bianca," called Vanilla, "and we'll teach you to float!" (Neither of the pretty creatures had ever learned to swim.) "Come in, and we'll dry you afterwards on our own saris!"

"Thank you, not at the moment," replied Miss Bianca gravely. "There are times for one sort of thing — such as learning to float — and times for another sort — such as serious conversation."

Like all frivolous natures, Muslin and Vanilla delighted in the idea of serious conversation. Instantly they were hanging like a couple of mermaids to the marble rim at her feet. — Vanilla still couldn't help kicking a little, to splash a spray of water over Muslin's shoulders, nor could Muslin refrain from splashing Vanilla back. Miss Bianca perceived in short that if she was to get any sense out of them, she must first make the strongest impression possible upon their gentle yet essentially silly minds. She thought rapidly; and like a good general

adopted the strategic rather than the tactical approach, which means that instead of at once tackling them on the subject of the page boy, she sought to impose her authority first.

"Good Muslin, good Vanilla," said Miss Bianca, "the time has come to be frank with you: I am not what I seem!"

The result of this impressive statement was rather unexpected. Muslin looked at Vanilla, Vanilla looked at Muslin, then both clapped their hands and burst into peals of delighted laughter.

"We always knew you weren't — didn't we, Muslin?" cried Vanilla. "We always *knew* you weren't really a mouse, but some enchanted princess under a spell cast by a wicked magician! Only you were so good and beautiful —"

"And sweet and kind —" put in Muslin.

"— he couldn't turn you into a frog —"

"As they usually do!" put in Muslin.

"— only into the prettiest little creature alive! No wonder you need to talk to us seriously! Do, do, darling Miss Bianca — or should we say your Royal Highness? — tell us just what we must do," finished Vanilla, "to help you break the spell!"

With which the pair salaamed as deeply as they could in a swimming pool, and tried to kiss her hand. Since it was so small, they ended by kissing her all over until she was quite damp.

"Oh, dear!" thought Miss Bianca. "Both obviously brought up on the *Arabian Nights!*" — and though their supposition was thus perhaps natural, and certainly flattering, it is always a delicate matter to explain, without causing disappointment, that instead of being an enchanted princess one is merely the head of a welfare organization. Miss Bianca however saw that she must do so at once, ere misunderstanding thickened like cream into cheese.

"Good Muslin, good Vanilla," she repeated, "let me assure you that in one sense I am quite exactly what I am — that is, a mouse from birth. — In fact with a pedigree long as your Ranee's," smiled Miss Bianca, "from my ancestress Blanche de Port Salut! I also, however, have the honor to fill the position of Perpetual Madam President of the Mouse Prisoners' Aid Society."

Fortunately, to Muslin and Vanilla this sounded almost as unusual as being an enchanted princess — indeed *more* unusual; there was nothing about Prisoners' Aid Societies in the *Arabian Nights*. Miss Bianca, seeing their looks of even deeper interest, felt she could come to the point.

"Thus you may still be of the greatest help," continued Miss Bianca, "if not in releasing me from any spell, in assisting me in my present function — beginning by telling me the truth and not simply what you may think I want to hear. Remember our previous conversation on the topic: consider before you reply: there *was,* wasn't there, at least *one* page boy in the Ranee's service?"

She was prepared to wait several minutes, while the pair considered; but Vanilla answered at once.

"Why, whatever put *that* into your head, darling Miss Bianca-if-not-your-Royal-Highness-Perpetual-Madam-President?" exclaimed Vanilla, with apparently genuine curiosity.

"I have been talking to a peacock," said Miss Bianca.

"Then you've been talking to a perfect bird-brain!" declared Vanilla. "Besides, what can peacocks know about it? In the first place they live outside — don't they, Muslin? A peacock hasn't a clue about what goes on in the Palace!"

Just what the peacock had said, reflected Miss Bianca, of Muslin and Vanilla! Who was telling the truth? She in turn began to feel she hadn't a clue, when every single informant, starting with Ali, came to appear so unreliable!

Evidently her drooping whiskers involuntarily betrayed her distressful emotions, for Vanilla and Muslin immediately began kissing her again.

"Don't, please, darling Miss Bianca-if-not-your-Royal-Highness-Perpetual-Madam-President, look so sad!" begged Vanilla. "The Ranee might see and be offended!"

"And if she is," began Muslin fearfully, "might even —"

"Hush!" interrupted Vanilla. "And don't *you* start looking sad either! Didn't darling Willow always teach us never to look sad?"

"Also to neither observe nor remember," suggested Miss Bianca, in her impatience splitting an infinitive. "My dear girls, for once in your lives *think!*"

Muslin burst into tears.

"I'm sorry if I spoke harshly —" resumed Miss Bianca.

"It's not *that!*" sobbed Muslin. "It's —"

"Don't think of it!" said Vanilla quickly.

"But I have!" wailed Muslin. "I *have,* Vanilla, and I know you have too!"

Vanilla began to cry as well. Clinging to each other in the water, they cried and cried . . .

"Really this is excessive," said Miss Bianca. "If you have indeed misinformed me, perhaps owing to some genuine lapse of memory, let us hope 'tis not too late to make amends without breaking your hearts first. I have been making a few calculations: only at full moon, I gather, are sentences actually carried out; therefore since according to Ali the boy's offense occurred some three weeks ago — that is, just after the *last* full moon, not until *this*, the night after next —"

"The night after next!" sobbed Vanilla.

"— is he in absolute peril of his life. There is thus still time to save him," continued Miss Bianca briskly, "though no time to be lost; so for goodness' sake stop crying and give me all relevant information you can."

But Vanilla and Muslin only sobbed the louder — until at last, and barely gasping the words out —

"You don't *know*, Miss Bianca!" choked Muslin. "We've tried not to let *ourselves* know! It's darling *Willow* who's in the elephant lines!"

3

For a moment Miss Bianca was so surprised, shocked and horrified, she was bereft of speech. — Yet was it not true, she now recalled, that for several days past Willow had been missing from the throne-room? — the absence of her sympathetic face indeed quite affecting Miss Bianca's touch on the harp? Yet how to credit such a dreadful circumstance?

"Willow?" repeated Miss Bianca. "Good, kind, conscientious Willow? How could *she* ever come to deserve such punishment?"

"Don't you remember?" sobbed Vanilla. "She *whispered* . . ."

"The night the poet rhymed lily wrong," wept Muslin.

"And Her Highness said it was very bad manners," sobbed Vanilla.

"So now she's in the elephant lines," wept Muslin, "and the full moon's only two nights off, and though I *know*, Vanilla — it was you who said her name first! — she wouldn't want us to think about her being trampled to smithereens, I *have* — and so have you — and oh, Miss Bianca, there's simply nothing we can do!"

"Perhaps not *you*," said Miss Bianca, already in full repossession of her faculties, "but 'tis a type of situation, however poignant, I am reasonably familiar with . . ."

4

All her compassion, indignation and prisoner-rescuing instincts rose to meet the challenge. The page boy might have existed, or he mightn't: between Ali and the peacock on one hand, and Bernard and Muslin and Vanilla on the other, Miss Bianca still wasn't sure; but Willow undoubtedly existed, also Miss Bianca entertained both liking and respect for her.

"Since time is so short, one must begin *at the other end*," said Miss Bianca decisively. "That is, by speaking a personal word to Hathi."

"Only no one ever *can* speak a personal word to him," mourned Vanilla. "He's so precious, and valuable, and worth his weight in gold, he's never let stir out without his mahout on his back!"

"I don't suppose his mahout, or driver, spends the whole night there?" said Miss Bianca. "Once within the elephant lines by night —"

"Only no one can get *into* the elephant lines!" despaired Muslin. "They're too heavily guarded!"

"I know of at least one certain way of gaining entrance," smiled Miss Bianca. "By offending the Ranee . . ."

Muslin and Vanilla almost fainted with dismay. Fond as they were of their darling Willow, they were by this time equally fond of their darling Miss Bianca.

"Oh, Miss Bianca, *you* think," cried Vanilla, "of what *your* dreadful fate may be!"

"Phooey," said Miss Bianca. (She didn't usually employ such vulgar expressions, also was well aware of the danger she courted, but wished to startle Muslin and Vanilla, for their own sakes, from looking so unhappy.) "Phooey!" repeated Miss Bianca. "I shall offend Her Highness this very evening!"

10. Into the Jaws of Elephants!

SHE WAS AS good as her word. She had played "Green-sleeves" once, "Le Camembert" twice: as the Ranee demanded a third rendering of that delightful air —

"I'm so sorry," said Miss Bianca, "I'm too tired."

She rose from the harp. For a moment there was such silence, the last twang of a golden string seemed to re-echo on the air. Muslin and Vanilla put their arms round each other.

"Too tired to play for *Her Highness?*" gasped one of the ladies at last.

"Of course I'm dreadfully sorry," said Miss Bianca lightly — so lightly that she didn't really sound sorry at all.

The Ranee's beautiful swallow-wing eyebrows drew together in a frown. Vanilla and Muslin clung closer still, while all the rest of the ladies tried to hide behind each other's backs.

"Be careful you don't offend me," said the Ranee. "You know what happens to people who offend me?"

"As I understand," said Miss Bianca, "they're sent to the elephant lines to be trampled to smithereens. But

99

really in my present state of fatigue *anything* is preferable to playing 'Le Camembert' again. In fact, I won't."

A sigh like wind over reeds shook the whole court. But none, to Miss Bianca's surprise, sighed louder than the Ranee!

"I think you're being very inconsiderate," complained the Ranee, "to force my hand so. Of course I always knew you'd have to be retired eventually, but I meant to have you stuffed. Trampled by Hathi, there wouldn't be a morsel left of your nice coat!"

"Look rather on the bright side," encouraged Miss Bianca. "I don't believe I should stuff at all well — and you wouldn't wish me preserved looking less than my best?"

"Oh, as to that," said the Ranee, "my taxidermist is quite *brilliant*. You should see how beautifully he did the cockatoos! Really they look far more handsome than in life."

"But consider the difference in size," pointed out Miss Bianca. "Cockatoos are practically poultry-sized; any competent cook could stuff a cockatoo." (Though she regretted speaking so disrespectfully of her ex-landlords, she felt that in the circumstances they would understand and forgive.) "To stuff a mouse," continued Miss Bianca, "is so much more fiddling; as I'm sure any taxidermist would find."

Unfortunately this plausible argument met an equally plausible rejoinder.

"*My* taxidermist," observed the Ranee, "can stuff hummingbirds — only look at that sweet little row of them holding up my gauze! I'm sure he'd make something really artistic of you; perhaps seated at the harp. In fact," concluded the Ranee, "and even though it means breaking with precedent, you *shan't* be sent to the elephant lines; you shall be drowned — without damage to a single hair! And just to show how merciful I am," she added, "in rose-water in a silver bowl, and by your two particular friends Muslin and Vanilla."

What could Miss Bianca do but bow her appreciation? (Vanilla and Muslin, despite Willow's teaching, barely restrained their tears.)

"Not only merciful, but thoughtful," said Miss Bianca. "After such kind consideration I only hope I may stuff quite exquisitely!" She paused. "All the same," she reflected, "shouldn't we wait but another day, for the full moon? — since I understand that only at her plenitude are such sentences customarily executed?"

"No, we shouldn't," said the Ranee. "*This* next full moon doesn't rise till midnight,* so it's far *more* than a day, and in any case I'm never to be kept waiting a minute. Someone fetch a bowl of rose-water!"

Miss Bianca shrugged.

"Just as you like," said she. "But though your Highness, out of the goodness of your Highness's heart, may be prepared to break with *one* precedent, is it not ever rash, in Royalty, to depart from protocol altogether?"

* Actually the full moon normally rises about sunset, but this happened to be that rarity a blue one. Hence the expression "once in a blue moon."

By protocol Miss Bianca meant the usual way of doing things at Courts, any departure from which might attract the notice of the populace and start it wondering whether Courts were really worthwhile. — The Ranee, who in her own selfish way was quite clever, paused in turn; then bade Muslin and Vanilla, instead of drowning Miss Bianca at once, to keep her in strict custody a day and a half longer; also promised to give a little party amongst intimates to witness the pretty ceremony planned.

2

"Dear me, how tiresome!" said Miss Bianca.

Vanilla, in the act of popping her tenderly into strict custody in Chez Cockatoo, gazed in tearful admiration.

"I don't know how you can be so brave, Miss Bianca," marveled Vanilla. "I suppose it comes with practice; for I'm sure Muslin and I couldn't call it just *tiresome,* if *we* were going to be drowned in rose-water. Even having to drown *you* in rose-water is too, too dreadful — isn't it, Muslin?"

"My dear girls," said Miss Bianca, "by 'tiresome' I referred not to the prospect of my immediate if fragrant death, which I can assure you is most unlikely to occur, but to the temporary hitch in my design. However, if the Ranee won't send me to the elephant lines, I must think of some other means of entering them, and in fact have done so already. You shall take me there yourselves."

Muslin looked at Vanilla. Vanilla looked at Muslin. It was as if the same shudder shook them both.

"But we can't, Miss Bianca! We don't know the way!" protested Muslin.

"Of course you do," said Miss Bianca briskly. "After so long in the Palace, of course you must know at least the *way* to the elephant lines, even if you haven't actually visited them."

"It's through the big arch beyond the stables," admitted Vanilla.

"Which since Bernard has no difficulty in getting here *from,* there can be no difficulty in getting from here *to,*" said Miss Bianca. " 'Tis true it takes him half a day, but to you 'twould be no more than half an hour; and as there's no time to lose I must ask you to carry me there at once. Only be brave —"

"Only we *aren't!*" cried Vanilla desperately. "We just *aren't* brave — are we, Muslin?"

There was no need for Muslin's affirmative nod. If Vanilla was shuddering again, Muslin's teeth were now positively chattering. Never had Miss Bianca encountered such a brace of poltroons! Then suddenly the recollection stirred of how little courageous she'd been herself, the first time she'd embarked on a heroic enterprise. When Bernard — how long ago! — first came to ask her help in rescuing a Norwegian poet from the Black Castle, hadn't the now famous intrepid Miss Bianca actually fainted from terror? And how had she been persuaded to undertake that enterprise? By an appeal not to her courage, but to her compassion . . .

"My dears," said Miss Bianca, in her sweetest and most

silvery tones, "as Vanilla just said, being brave, like playing the harp, comes only by practice. Why shouldn't you both begin to practice now — especially in the interest of your darling Willow?"

This appeal too was not without effect. Even a chickenheart may be also a truly fond one.

"Darling Willow!" murmured Vanilla.

"Darling Willow!" echoed Muslin.

"Who held your hands," reminded Miss Bianca, "when you were so young you cried in bed . . ."

Vanilla looked at Muslin; Muslin looked at Vanilla; while Miss Bianca waited anxiously — because if *they* wouldn't carry her to the elephant lines, however was she to get there in time? Then suddenly, in the same sniff —

"We'll try!" sniffed Muslin and Vanilla.

3

Undoubtedly it was a splendid start at being brave, to carry Miss Bianca out into and across the palace gardens. Fortunately it wasn't dark — both Muslin and Vanilla were afraid of the dark — the moon being but a night from full; yet in a way this made things worse, since the party could be more easily observed by a patrolling watchman. But with their hearts in their mouths (and Miss Bianca in a fold of Vanilla's sari), they slipped from the shadow of one rosebush to the next, then into the shadow of a lilac-alley, and so gained the stables.

In a little snuggery under the harness-room floor Bernard was swapping jokes with his fellow polo-players. Little did he guess that Miss Bianca was so nigh, or what she was up to!

The stable watchman *did* observe them. Luckily he took Muslin and Vanilla, in their pale draperies, for two ghosts. He disappeared as swiftly as a ghost himself ere beyond, at last, loomed the huge granite archway.

It was heavily barred, but of course Miss Bianca could get through.

"Here set me down," said she. "And my dears, you've not only been brave, you've been positive heroines! Why, you needed no practice at all! — many a hero of antiquity could take a lesson from you!"

At this well-deserved praise, both beamed with such pride, pleasure, self-satisfaction (and why not?) and enthusiastic cooperativeness, no one would have taken them for the same girls who half an hour earlier could only shiver and shake! But such is often the result of trying.

"We'll wait for you till you get back," said Vanilla. "Won't we, Muslin?"

Miss Bianca gave each a kiss and slipped through the bars. She had often been in the jaws of death before (counting bloodhounds), but never yet in the jaws, or rather upon the tusks, of elephants. She advanced nonetheless with all her usual coolness in the jaws of anything.

11. Hathi

IMMEDIATELY, HOWEVER, Miss Bianca wondered whether her friends hadn't by mistake introduced her not into the elephant lines at all, but rather into the aisle of some great cathedral lined with double granite pillars on each side. As first one pillar, then the next, began to twitch and shift, Miss Bianca very much hoped there wasn't going to be an earthquake. Then she perceived that the base of each column had toenails on it — each to Miss Bianca big as a barn door, but undoubtedly toenails — and realized not only that what she'd taken for the supports of a sacred edifice were in fact the back legs of twenty or so elephants, but also that it was probably her own minuscule presence that made them tremble so. "I must certainly tell Bernard," thought Miss Bianca, "who has never really believed elephants to be afraid of mice, that I produced quite the effect of an earthquake!"

This wasn't strictly true, since it was she herself who had thought of earthquakes, not the elephants. But what was true was that all the elephants were nervous because they felt there was a mouse about, while Miss Bianca was so heartened, she ran on with ever-increasing confidence.

There was no sight of Willow. — This Miss Bianca had expected: obviously prisoners waiting to be trampled to smithereens wouldn't be held actually *in* the elephant lines — there wouldn't be accommodation, also the elephants might get fond of them — but in some adjacent prison; what she hadn't expected, however, was the total absence of guards. In fact the stable guard had loyally rushed to inform his colleagues that there were ghosts abroad, and all the elephant-line guards had vamoosed along with him to a safe distance. But though she didn't guess the reason, Miss Bianca was heartened afresh; and finally approached the very biggest elephant, Hathi, the Ranee's favorite, without having turned a whisker.

He was so big she couldn't see all of him at once. Miss Bianca still felt slightly like a tourist in a cathedral as she tiptoed between his back legs, then his front, admiring, so to speak, the architecture. When she ran up on his manger it was like confronting a stained-glass window! — for Hathi's trunk and forehead and ears alike were painted all over with patterns of scarlet and green. The aim of this decoration, when the Ranee rode out on his back, was to produce in the beholder not only admiration but awe: Miss Bianca however was too sophisticated to feel either of these emotions. She in fact thought Hathi would look better left in his native state of granite-grayness. Certainly she wasn't awed at all, but rather held herself ready to comfort and reassure should her sudden appearance at close quarters have the effect she now confidently anticipated. — It had. No sooner did he set eyes on her than the enormous pachyderm began quaking all over from the tip of his trunk to the root of his tail. His thick skin rippled like lava, his flanks heaved in and out. It was like seeing Vesuvius about to erupt, or an iceberg about to calve, or any other tremendous force of nature in violent convulsion.

"Go away! Don't come near me! Fetch my mahout!" squealed Hathi.

"Pray be under no apprehension!" said Miss Bianca. "I won't hurt you! All I seek is a little chat, and perhaps cooperation. — Though why any person of *your* size," she added curiously, "should be apprehensive of anyone mouse-size, I confess I find difficult to understand?"

"*You* weren't in the Ark," snuffled Hathi, calming down a bit, but still nervously.

"Nor you either, I suppose!" smiled Miss Bianca. "And surely whatever happened in the Ark is too long ago to bother about now?"

"An elephant never forgets," returned Hathi. "How a couple of mice, in the Ark, drove my I-don't-know-how-many-great-great-great-grandparents nearly overboard by playing hide-and-seek in their ears is something I for one shan't ever forget if I live to be old as Methuselah. — And it wasn't only us elephants who complained to Noah," he went on, now seeming quite pleased to have someone to talk, or rather grumble, to. "The zebras complained as well, about hopscotch on their stripes. There was quite a petition got up to Noah, to send those two *mice* swimming out to sea and see what *they'd* bring back, instead of nice inoffensive Mrs. Dove!"

Though it was a bad beginning, Miss Bianca collected her wits and employed all her well-known tact.

"I see you have good reason for your suspicions," she said soothingly, "and must really apologize on behalf of my whole race! But since those days I'm sure you'll find us grown better-mannered: in my *own* memory I can't recall a single instance of a mouse driving an elephant to near self-destruction in the way you so feelingly describe."

"I dare say *your* memory isn't very long," said Hathi unconvincedly. "I dare say there's been hundreds. In fact it's a thing I'd rather not discuss, because I happen to be very sensitive and tenderhearted to a fault."

At this Miss Bianca absolutely lost patience with him.

"An elephant, and you call yourself sensitive!" she exclaimed indignantly. "An elephant, and you call yourself tenderhearted — you who trample people to smithereens!"

To her astonishment, at these stinging words Hathi looked neither ashamed, nor angry, nor contrite, but simply and utterly astounded.

2

"Trample *people?*" he repeated incredulously. "Us elephants trample *people?* Goodness me, we'd never think of such a thing! A tiger, perhaps, in self-defense —"

"But you do, you know," said Miss Bianca. "I'm afraid it's only too well authenticated. You yourself are on record as having —" she shuddered delicately —" made puff-pastry of Her Highness's Head Pastry Cook."

"Whenever?" demanded Hathi indignantly.

"At last full moon," said Miss Bianca.

He thought for a moment; then looked relieved.

"Oh, *that!*" said Hathi. "Why, that was just a tidying-up job on the new airstrip. Some ill-conditioned person had left a great bundle of rubbish and so on bang in the middle, and I was asked if I'd mind just going along after hours to stamp it nice and flat. Of course a full moon always rather dazzles me; I just shut my eyes and stamped; but I do honestly assure you it was just a tidying-up job."

Alas, thought Miss Bianca, how even the best-hearted — for she felt sure Hathi was good at heart — could be misled into performing the cruelest actions, if only they were told they were doing something else and didn't look for themselves! " 'Tis how half the evil in the world is done," thought Miss Bianca sadly, "by the innocent to the innocent . . ." It struck her indeed that the Head Pastry Cook mightn't have been entirely innocent —

might have sold cakes on the side, or skimped and stolen the butter — such was the way of life at the Ranee's court! — but the thought brought no consolation; if he'd been a Christian martyr Hathi would have trampled him just the same, under the impression of doing something praiseworthy . . .

"I do hope you believe me?" pressed Hathi, evidently a little worried by her silence.

"Yes, indeed," said Miss Bianca. "I do indeed believe you, poor Hathi! In fact, at next full moon, actually to-morrow, in case there's any *more* rubbish to be tidied, it would give me pleasure to accompany you and watch in person. In the capital where I usually reside, rubbish-disposal is such a problem, I should be glad to pick up a few hints to transmit to the Municipal Authorities . . ."

She chose her words wisely. Big words like Municipal Authorities always impress an elephant.

"I should be honored," said Hathi. — A last uncontrollable shudder nonetheless rippled his hide. "When you say *accompany* me," he added nervously, "you don't mean *on* me?"

"Certainly I do," said Miss Bianca. (At ground-level on the airstrip, Hathi trampling conscientiously about, she'd probably have been the first casualty.) "As I remarked earlier, whatever occurred in the Ark is surely too long ago to affect our present relationship! Forget the Ark! — Hold out your trunk, let me run just once up and down it, and I'm sure you'll never be frightened of a mouse again!"

It quite amused Miss Bianca to think that after teaching Muslin and Vanilla to be brave, she was now teaching an elephant to be! But though this may sound absurd, it was actually the most courageous thing Hathi had ever achieved in his life, as after a moment's hesitation he did as Miss Bianca invited. He had often been courageous before, while he was still wild, fighting off tigers — but that was in hot blood, and in any case something expected of elephants. All his relations would have been ashamed of him if he hadn't fought courageously. Now he had to overcome not only an inherited fear of mice, but also the fear of what those same relations would say if they heard of his actually fraternizing with one. It called for a different kind of courage, the sort known as moral, and which is often harder to produce than the bang-and-bang-back sort. But under the influence of Miss Bianca's personality and eloquence, Hathi suddenly felt brave all round.

Miss Bianca was pretty brave too. Hathi's extended trunk swayed before her like a suspension-bridge; the red and green zigzags with which it was painted affected her as a motorist might have been affected by traffic-lights stuck simultaneously at Stop and Go. Summoning all her own poise and courage, however, she positively tripped, light as a feather, acoss the rubbery surface; paused a moment, to take breath, on the belvedere of Hathi's forehead, and as lightly tripped back without even making him sneeze.

"So you see," smiled Miss Bianca, "it wasn't so dreadful after all!"

"Actually it felt rather nice," confessed Hathi. "Like when Mummy used to stroke a headache away . . . You can come and ride on me whenever you like!"

"I shall take you at your word!" called Miss Bianca, as she scampered back towards the archway.

3

On its further side Muslin and Vanilla were waiting just as promised. They hadn't even been *bored,* they assured Miss Bianca; in fact (their frivolous natures reasserting themselves), they'd had a thoroughly enjoyable time pretending to be ghosts and going *Boo-hoo* to scare off any returning conscientious guard who showed his nose . . .

"If you'd only seen them," giggled Vanilla, scooping Miss Bianca up again, "when Muslin went *Boo-hoo-hoo!*"

Actually Miss Bianca hadn't time to recount her own experiences, as ere the party recrossed the stables they overtook Bernard making for Chez Cockatoo. It could have been quite a gay reunion, only Bernard obviously felt otherwise.

"If you wanted a look at the Stables, Miss Bianca," said he, in a huffish tone, "I'd have been only too happy to show you round myself. I've *wanted* to show you round, only I thought the trip might be too tiring."

"So it would indeed," agreed Miss Bianca. "Which is
why I have availed myself of Muslin and Vanilla's kind-
ness . . ."

"I still think you might have told me you were coming," said Bernard.

He sounded not only huffish but hurt. Miss Bianca ran
lightly down Vanilla's sari, to be able to talk to him face
to face instead of *de haut en bas*.

"I thought you'd be playing polo," she explained —
not quite truthfully, because in fact ever since hearing
of Willow's plight she'd been too preoccupied to give a
thought to Bernard at all. "Isn't it the Finals?"

"The Finals," said Bernard, "are tomorrow. In the
afternoon. That's why I started so early to come and see
you, so as to get back in time to get a bit of a rest first."

Miss Bianca was really touched. She knew how much the Finals meant to him — yet to visit her in Chez Cockatoo he had been prepared to spend almost the whole morning hiking!

"Dear Bernard," said she, "do pray forgive my foolish, female confusion! And since we happen to have met here and now, why not take advantage of the circumstance, and without foregoing our usual pleasant chat spare you further exertion? I'm sure our friends won't mind waiting a little longer!"

So speaking, she sank gracefully down on a nicely rounded cobblestone, and of course Bernard did the same, while Muslin and Vanilla amused themselves by draping the hems of their saris in a little surrounding tent. It was really just as cozy and private as at Chez Cockatoo.

"I'm sorry if I sounded cross," said Bernard.

" 'Twas only natural," said Miss Bianca. "And how good of you to contemplate the journey at all, in such circumstances!"

"Well, to be honest," said honest Bernard honestly, "I nearly didn't contemplate it, before the Final; only I specially wanted to tell you, something I overheard from that chauffeur, that the Ambassador's plane didn't leave last Tuesday after all. It leaves tomorrow midnight instead, and I thought you'd want us to take it."

'Twas the very news Miss Bianca needed, to enable her to extend her audacious plan for saving Willow's life into one for rescuing her altogether!

4

"Certainly we should take it!" exclaimed Miss Bianca. "Actually at midnight, you say?"

"Well, plus half an hour," said Bernard. "And I know what you're thinking, Miss Bianca, because I've thought of it myself: what a glorious sight it's going to be as up we soar in the light of the full moon!"

Of course Miss Bianca did thoroughly look forward to such a sight — but what she was actually thinking was that such a schedule allowed time to embark Willow on board the plane too!

"So I'll come and fetch you straightaway after the match," went on Bernard, "even if it means missing — whether we win or lose, though in my opinion it's a cert — a bit of a celebration. Just have your bag ready packed."

"Don't think of it," said Miss Bianca hastily. "Vanilla and Muslin will I'm sure again offer their services, so why not let us simply meet at the airstrip? In fact, I'll join you on the plane."

Bernard found this a very good idea. Besides sparing Miss Bianca fatigue, it meant he needn't miss the celebration, also several members of the polo team had promised to come and see him off, and he felt he wouldn't at all mind them seeing him, besides off, seen off by two such beauties as Muslin and Vanilla as well.

Little did he guess that Miss Bianca planned to gain the aircraft not at the pretty hands of ladies, but on ele-phant-back!

12. The Waiting Hours

Miss Bianca in fact never returned to Chez Cockatoo at all. As soon as Bernard had bidden her a fond (temporary) farewell —

"My dears," Miss Bianca told Muslin and Vanilla, "I have decided 'twill be wiser for me, during the next elapsing hours, to shun the Palace altogether. My conversation with Hathi has been fruitful indeed; there is every hope of Willow's safety; but I cannot risk Her Highness's suddenly jumping the gun and ordering me drowned in rose-water ahead of time. I therefore propose to return with you no further than the garden-limit, where in some rustic nook to wait out the day. In short, my dears, this is where we part."

For a wonder — or perhaps it wasn't such a wonder, now that they'd learnt to be brave — neither Muslin nor Vanilla burst into tears.

"We always knew you'd vanish sometime — didn't we, Muslin?" sighed Vanilla.

"As enchanted princesses always do!" sighed Muslin. (She at least, however newly brave, still under the influence of the *Arabian Nights*.) "But isn't there anything we can fetch you, Miss Bianca, like light lunch or your overnight bag?"

Miss Bianca hesitated. For luncheon she had no doubt of finding a sprig of wild parsley — notoriously full of vitamins — to nibble, whereas her overnight bag she was really attached to. But a point much on her mind was the consequences to her friends when the Ranee found the centerpiece, so to speak, of a little intimate drowning-party lacking . . . After a moment's thought, Miss Bianca slipped the emerald ring from about her neck and deposited it beside Vanilla's toes.

"The Ranee's jewel," said Miss Bianca, "I leave as a gift between you. I know you won't quarrel over it! But will it suffice, should the Ranee turn her anger upon you, to bribe your way to freedom out of the elephant lines?"

Vanilla looked at Muslin. Muslin looked at Vanilla.

"Actually," confessed Vanilla, "we've often thought — haven't we, Muslin? — of all sorts of things we could do with it. Muslin has an uncle who's a jeweler —"

"And Vanilla has an uncle who's a farmer —" put in Muslin.

"And if we sold it to Muslin's uncle, and took a whole bag of gold back to *my* uncle, we could marry the two handsomest boys in my uncle's village! We've even thought of how we could get away — by putting on quite shabby saris and mixing with the cowherds who come at dawn to bring milk. But until you've now taught us to be brave, Miss Bianca, we'd never have done it!"

"And anyway we hadn't *got* the emerald," pointed out Muslin, with unexpected practicality. "You do really and truly, Miss Bianca, give it us?"

"With all my heart!" declared Miss Bianca. — "See, dawn begins to break already," she added, "and I'm sure your saris, after such a night's adventuring, look quite shabby enough as it is! Take the jewel and run as fast as you can, my dears, join the cowherds without delay, and don't give another thought to my overnight bag!"

Muslin and Vanilla at once obeyed her instructions. — Vanilla stooped for the emerald ring and tied it in a corner of her sari, letting Muslin hold the knot, then they kissed Miss Bianca most fervently, and ran as fast as they

could to mingle with the cowherds, and so no more than Miss Bianca ever returned to the Ranee's cruel palace.

2

At the garden-limit weeds rioted. Miss Bianca had no difficulty in finding herself a hammock among convolvuluses wherein to doze out the rest of the day ere midnight, with all its attendant perils, loomed — and what better interim resource than poetry?

POEM BY MISS BIANCA
COMPOSED WHILE WAITING TO BOARD
AN AIRPLANE BY ELEPHANT

Rocking to and fro, to and fro, to and fro

murmured Miss Bianca to herself,

Rocking to and fro, where the big blue blossoms blow —

"*I*'d say, 'on the go,' " remarked a passing bee. "*I'm* always on the go!"

"Indeed quite a proverb for it," said Miss Bianca, rather shortly. "Don't let me detain you!"

"*Swinging high and low, high and low, high and low,*"

she continued,

"Swinging high and low, where the tall grasses grow
In the shade unafraid of the sun!"

She hadn't realized there was a lizard so close.

"You've got it the wrong way round," criticized the lizard. "It ought to be 'in the *sun* unafraid of the *shade!*' "

Miss Bianca was unused to composing poetry so to speak in public, and after this second interruption went on inside her head.

> *No sweeter spot to wait in,*
> *Relax and meditate in,*
> *Till the long hours of waiting have run!*
>
> M. B.

She composed several other verses, all in the same lulling rhythm, and in fact halfway through the fifth had lulled herself to sleep. Which was just as well, considering her exertions of the previous night, also what exertions lay before her!

Miss Bianca in fact slept until past sundown, and long after that; absolutely until the skies lightened with adumbrant moonrise . . .

"Good gracious!" thought Miss Bianca, hurrying back across the stables, "what if I had overslept! How many a slip there is indeed, betwixt cup and lip!"

She spoke more prophetically than she knew!

13. The Cup and the Lip

Beyond the archway into the elephant lines there seemed to be a good deal of activity. Hathi was out of his stall, his driver already mounted, while in the other stalls other mahouts moved nervously about trying to keep their elephants quiet. As all down the lines trunks quivered and tails switched, 'twas less like being in a cathedral, thought Miss Bianca, than in a forest with a storm blowing up . . .,

"And I don't believe 'tis on my account either!" thought she — but not with any offended vanity; she was only too glad to be able to run up and take station behind Hathi's left ear unobserved. Even his mahout, an elderly, grim-faced man, didn't observe her; in fact he had an oddly drowsy look that for a moment suggested to Miss Bianca that perhaps he'd been refreshing himself with something stronger than either coffee or sherbet; then she charitably put it down to the lateness of the hour.

"Here I am!" whispered Miss Bianca, into the great big-as-a-banana-leaf ear-flap. (Painted now, she observed, not with red and green but black and purple. So were his trunk and forehead painted in the same funereal colors.)

"I began to think you'd forgotten," mumbled Hathi. "And I still can't think why you want to come along on just a little tidying-up job . . ."

"Call it feminine caprice," said Miss Bianca. "You who so often carry the Ranee must surely know what *that* means!"

"Mostly being kow-towed to in bazaars," mumbled Hathi. "However, if *your* caprice is to watch me doing sweeper's work, hold tight!"

With that he swung into the long, rocking elephant-stride that affects some passengers like the motion of a ship at sea. But Miss Bianca had been to sea, and knew just how to keep balance. As Hathi lunged first to port, then to starboard, she preserved all her customary aplomb, both mental and physical.

Only how brilliant and startling rose the Oriental full moon! More startling still because slightly blue! Even through her thick dark lashes Miss Bianca was almost dazzled, while she felt quite sure Hathi was.

There were other illuminations. As they approached the new airstrip, on the old one adjoining Miss Bianca could see the lights of the plane that presumably had the Oriental Ambassador, also Bernard, already on board. Besides seeing, she could hear; and across the short distance, what she feared she heard was the sound of its propellers experimentally revving up . . .

Hathi paused to ask if she was quite comfortable.

"Perfectly!" said Miss Bianca. "Pray don't go slowly on my account! In fact, couldn't you hurry a little?"

But nothing can make an elephant hurry when he doesn't want to, and evidently Hathi wasn't wanting to. On he rocked a few strides more, then paused again.

"I don't know why," mumbled Hathi, "but somehow I just don't feel like trampling tonight. Anyway, *I* can't see any rubbish lying about."

Naturally, thought Miss Bianca, moon-dazzled as he was! Or could it be a subconscious bad conscience suddenly operating? ("If so, how untimely!" thought Miss Bianca.) But *she* could see, and what she saw made her throw into her next words all the persuasiveness and urgency possible.

"Good Hathi, do pray proceed!" begged Miss Bianca. "For in the airstrip's very center *I* perceive some obstruction indeed!"

"Oh, all right!" grumbled Hathi, "but I may as well do it with my eyes shut and just let old Surly guide me!"

On he lumbered again towards the center of the airstrip; where lay besides the bound-hand-and-foot figure of Willow *a bound-hand-and-foot little boy in tatters of white and cherry-colored silk!*

As his mahout halted him —

"This the place?" muttered Hathi.

"Yes!" screamed Miss Bianca, running down his trunk and beginning to nibble feverishly at the bonds. "Yes, yes, yes, Hathi! The place, and the *people* — whom, instead of trampling, you shall bear to safety! Open your eyes and gather us up!"

"Shan't," said Hathi, with a sudden return of obstinacy. "In fact, I shan't do anything more at all. I shall just stop as I am, and go to sleep until I feel the sun nice and hot on my back in the morning . . ."

Not Miss Bianca's renewed pleas could stir him, nor the mahout's cruel goad, as there stood Hathi indifferent and immovable while the propellers revved up for the last time . . .

2

The aircraft was all set to go. The Captain, with the few minutes in hand he always allowed himself, was taking a last stroll and a last few gulps of fresh air. So was the Air Hostess, a little way behind.

Bernard, who couldn't imagine what had happened to Miss Bianca, was so desperate he tried to run back down the gangway, only his enthusiastic supporters from the Mouse Oriental Polo Club got in the way. He was actually at fisticuffs with them, but heavily outnumbered.

The Captain turned back. In exactly three minutes he would be in his seat at the controls and Miss Fitzpatrick heating tinned soup and the aircraft airborne — and Miss Bianca and Willow and the page boy irretrievably left behind!

3

Suddenly the Captain halted.

"Good heavens!" he exclaimed. "What is this I see?"

Well might he exclaim! There in front of the propellers the mustard-and-cress sown by Miss Bianca had sprouted in three universally recognized letters . . .

"I say, Miss Fitzpatrick!" called the Captain, "just come and take a look at this! Do you see what I see?"

"Certainly," said the hostess. "It's a mustard-and-cress. I've sown it myself, for my baby brother's initials."

"Perhaps one of the locals," suggested the Captain, "has a baby brother named Selim Ozmandias Sennacherib?"

But he spoke more lightly than he felt, and Miss Fitzpatrick knew it. The letters *might* represent the initials of a Selim Ozmandias Sennacherib: what they did beyond doubt represent was the universally recognized signal meaning HELP! — exactly as Miss Bianca had intended they should when she sowed them on the very moment of arrival, just in case.

"S.O.S.," said the Captain uneasily.

"S.O.S. it is," agreed Miss Fitzpatrick.

"Everyone aboard all right?" asked the Captain. "No one left behind?"

"If they were, they'd hardly have time to grow mustard-and-cress," said Miss Fitzpatrick practically. "Anyway, I've seen the Ambassador into his berth and ticked off every member of his suite. All the same —"

"All the same?" prompted the Captain.

"All the same," suggested the Hostess, "mightn't we wait just a few minutes longer, and catch up over the Indian Ocean?"

4

Thus it was that the plane still hadn't taken off when Miss Bianca employed her last desperate resource and by a sharp nip on the tender tip of Hathi's trunk managed to rouse him from his selfish somnolence. — It was purely from pain that he opened his eyes; but when he did, and saw not rubbish but human forms lying in his path, his remorse and anger knew no bounds.

"This is awful!" Hathi trumpeted his distress abroad. "I've been deceived!" — With a furious shrug he chucked the mahout clean off his back. "Us elephants don't trample *people!* Or if I ever have by mistake, only tell me what I can do now to make amends!"

Miss Bianca told him at once. Down and aloft wreathed Hathi's trunk, scooping up Willow and the page boy and Miss Bianca, ere he braced himself for the charge!

5

"If you see what I see," said the Air Hostess, with her customary calm, "there seems to be an elephant charging us. He's not on the list; should I try to berth him amidships?"

"Good heavens, we'd never get off the ground!" cried the Captain. "Fetch his Excellency at once and tell him absolutely no zoological specimens allowed! — No, there isn't time," decided the Captain. "Just stand clear of the doors, Miss Fitzpatrick, and gangway up!"

14. The End

BUT WHAT WAS a chuck of a few yards to an elephant? With an easy twirl of his powerful trunk Hathi gently lofted in his three passengers just ere the cabin door closed, then rumbled a courteous farewell to Miss Bianca, and swayed back under the moonlight to his own quarters. Contrary to Miss Fitzpatrick's and the Captain's apprehensions, he'd never intended boarding the plane himself; it looked to him too much like a Noah's Ark.

2

Now it was that the Air Hostess's wonderful qualities showed at their best — that is, she completely disregarded all regulations about not taking passengers on board without tickets. Confronted by two obviously suffering fellow creatures — Willow and the page boy — Miss Fitzpatrick simply put them in the two nearest empty seats and adjusted their safety-belts. (There were plenty of empty seats, since only the Ambassador and his suite were officially traveling.) Then she splashed Willow with lavender-water, popped a barley-sugar sweet into the page boy's mouth, and opened two more tins of soup. The one thing Miss Fitzpatrick didn't do was make her way forward and report to the Captain, since any ignoring of the regulations on *his* part might well cost him his Captaincy, and she had his interests truly at heart.

"Sleep as long as you can, poor lady!" murmured Miss Fitzpatrick to Willow, as she finally flicked the cabin lights off. "And you too, you poor little urchin! I'll not trouble you with cleaning up till morning! — Now don't tell me it's the pair of *you* here again!" she added, with a change of tone, as entering her own private cubicle there she saw Bernard and Miss Bianca sitting side by side on her box of Kleenex . . .

3

Their reunion had been rather tempestuous. Naturally the nerves of both were a little on edge, and their tempers a little frayed: to Miss Bianca's cold inquiry as to why Bernard had so nearly let the aircraft leave without her, Bernard had hotly replied that people who preferred to catch an airplane by elephant should at least employ punctual elephants; also that the very moment he realized her overdue, he'd tried to scrum down to look for her through practically the whole Mouse Oriental Polo Club.

"In fact brawling," said Miss Bianca coldly. "Good Hathi I admit may have been a little dilatory —"

"The big brute!" snarled Bernard.

"— but how effectual his aid at last!" pointed out Miss

Bianca. "Never mind, my dear Bernard; here I am, thanks to Hathi, safe and sound!"

"But I do mind!" cried Bernard. "It should have been thanks to me! — O Miss Bianca, if you only knew what agonies I went through (besides the members of the Mouse Oriental Polo Club), when for several dreadful moments I thought perhaps we'd never see each other again! I began to tear my whiskers out by the roots! — Just look, Miss Bianca!" cried Bernard. "It was my very longest!"

There indeed it lay between them on the Kleenex — Bernard's longest whisker. How could Miss Bianca, who knew what pride he'd taken in it — Bernard's whiskers, as has been remarked, were much stronger on strength than length — fail to accept such evidence of his true concern for her? She couldn't. Gently stroking the poor uprooted member, she actually bestowed upon it a tear. Bernard hastily folded it in his spotted handkerchief to keep it damp as long as possible, and thus peace and mutual understanding settled over the Kleenex like a refreshing dew and the Air Hostess had no idea of what a tempestuous scene she came in on the end of.

"This time neither the one of you even labeled!" said Miss Fitzpatrick resignedly. "Very well; you must just shift for yourselves and pick up whatever crumbs going, for I've enough on my hands as it is. — At least you don't require passports," she added, "and where on earth I'm to disembark passengers *without* passports I only wish I could ask my granny!"

Actually Miss Bianca had been struck by the same point; so a couple of hours later, while everyone else was deep in sleep, she slipped from the Hostess's cubicle and made her way to the Oriental Ambassador's V.I.P. reserved seat.

How tired he looked, the poor Oriental Ambassador! — dressed not now in cloth-of-gold but in a rather crumpled linen suit, and with his tie hanging slack from his loosened collar! He hadn't even taken his shoes off; evidently he'd fallen asleep while still trying to read all the papers that spilled from his briefcase over the blanket provided by the Air Line. *"Irrigation"* Miss Bianca saw one headed, and another, *"Agricultural Implements."* It quite went to her heart to rouse him, but she had to, if she was to spare Willow and the page boy the disagreeableness of having to spend the rest of their lives airborne.

"Pray forgive me," said she, as at the brush of her whiskers the Ambassador opened sleep-heavy eyes. "Only on a matter of extreme urgency would I have disturbed your well-earned repose!"

Half-asleep as he was, the Ambassador recognized her.

"That charming face have I not seen before," he murmured, with a smile, "peeping from a boy's pocket?"

"Good gracious!" said Miss Bianca, much flattered. "I didn't intend your Excellency to notice me!"

"Then it would have been my loss," the Ambassador assured her gallantly, "for to me you provided the grace-note of the whole evening! I only wish I'd known you envisaged a trip to the Orient; I might have had the privilege of escorting you out as well as back."

Of course in a sense he *had* escorted her out; however the point was too complicated to explain to an Ambassador only half-awake. Even as he went on to express a courteous hope that she'd enjoyed herself, it was through a yawn — which Miss Bianca as courteously ignored.

"Quite immensely," said she. "Not only was my ambition to stroke a peacock at last fulfilled, but I also rode an elephant. My immediate concern with your Excellency, however, is to beg your Excellency to make out a couple of passports in the names of M. (for Madam) Willow, and B. (for Boy) Page."

Half in a dream, the Ambassador did so. — It was Miss Bianca who found the proper sheets of paper for him, out of his briefcase, also the big official stamp upon which she sat down herself to make the proper official impression. Then she carried the precious documents back with her, and slipped one into the hands of M. Willow and the other into B. Page's sash, where the Air Hostess found them next morning.

"Goodness me!" thought Miss Fitzpatrick. "So they've passports after all! However did I fail to notice? Now I can at least disembark them at the first stop — which isn't it where you two got on?" she added, to Miss Bianca and Bernard. "Then you shall all disembark together," she decided, "and good luck go with you!'"

But first she helped Willow and the page boy to make themselves clean and tidy, and lent to each one of her own neat overalls, and thus with their passports in their hands they followed the line through the Customs quite easily. To make things easier still, there just outside was Miss Bianca's own Ambassador come to wave a greeting to his colleague, and who, being the kindest man in the world, when he saw two strangers standing obviously nervous and bewildered, took them back in his car to the Embassy to be sorted out. Of course Bernard and Miss Bianca got in too, and making themselves small on the floor sat so close together their whiskers were practically brushing. — If he'd still had his longest, Bernard felt, they actually would have brushed; but since it was his sacrifice of it that had stopped Miss Bianca being cross with him he didn't regret the circumstance, especially as he had it wrapped in his spotted handkerchief to take out and look at.

What a happy reunion it was, between Miss Bianca and her own Boy in the Embassy schoolroom! — Miss Bianca regaining the Pagoda just in time to welcome him back as in he burst from summer camp scattering fishing rods, baseball bats, tennis rackets and boxing gloves in every direction! The Boy's first hug was for his mother; then he hugged Miss Bianca almost to suffocation!

"You haven't been too lonely and bored, Miss Bianca?" he inquired anxiously. "Next year I'll take you with me! — but I do hope you haven't been *too* bored?"

Miss Bianca but smiled a diplomatic smile!

4

B. Page was adopted as a nephew by the Boy's tutor, who already had one nephew living with him, and kindly said the more the merrier, and all did lessons together.

Willow turned out to be exactly the sort of person needed at the local Orphanage to teach music, embroidery and consideration for others. Under her beneficent influence all the orphans grew up so charming, they married the moment they were old enough, and so became no longer orphans — a husband counting as family.

The Captain of the aircraft and Miss Fitzpatrick got married as soon as they had a week's leave together, and lived happy ever after, as did Muslin and Vanilla with the two handsomest boys in Vanilla's uncle's village.

Hathi, now that his eyes were opened, positively refused to do any more trampling, nor, under his leadership, would any of the other elephants, and the cruel custom quite died out.

The silk pavilion in the Pagoda grounds was a great success, especially during that winter, which was exceptionally severe. As Bernard had foreseen, Miss Bianca could sit out of doors in it, catching any sunshine going, and remain perfectly warm and snug; and Bernard often shared the privilege, talking about polo. A particularly delightful circumstance was that this very spot, or pouch, in which the whole adventure began, proved to have been embroidered by Willow herself!

The faithless Ali was never seen again. Sometimes the conservatory-gardener fancied he glimpsed the tip of a green tail, but it was always a curling tendril, or swaying stem, or drooping fern-frond; and whether the Ambassadorial conservatory still has a snakeling in it is unknown to this day.

THE END

MS READ-a-thon—
a simple way to start youngsters reading

Boys and girls between 6 and 14 can join the MS READ-a-thon and help find a cure for Multiple Sclerosis by reading books. And they get two rewards — the enjoyment of reading, and the great feeling that comes from helping others.

Parents and educators: For complete information call your local MS chapter. Or mail the coupon below.

Kids can help, too!

Beverly Cleary

Her books make kids laugh out loud!

YEARLING BOOKS

- ☐ ELLEN TEBBITS $2.25 (42299-X)
- ☐ EMILY'S RUNAWAY IMAGINATION...................................$2.50 (42215-9)
- ☐ MITCH AND AMY $2.25 (45411-5)
- ☐ THE MOUSE AND THE MOTORCYCLE.................................$2.25 (46075-1)
- ☐ OTIS SPOFFORD $1.95 (46651-2)
- ☐ RIBSY...$2.25 (47456-6)
- ☐ RUNAWAY RALPH $2.25 (47519-8)
- ☐ SOCKS...$2.50 (48256-9)

Tales of adventure through time and space
MADELEINE L'ENGLE

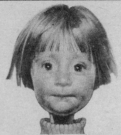

Beverly Cleary

Her little heroine, Ramona Quimby, is

IRRESISTIBLE!

Read about this winsome and winning girl wonder who's become one of the most popular kids on the block.

_____BEEZUS AND RAMONA.......$2.50 (40665-X)

_____RAMONA AND HER
FATHER $2.50 (47241-5)

_____RAMONA AND HER
MOTHER $2.25 (47243-1)

_____RAMONA QUIMBY, AGE 8....$2.25 (47350-0)

_____RAMONA THE PEST.............$2.50 (47209-1)

YEARLING BOOKS